JOIN THE FLUB

THE WORST DETECTIVE EVER

CHRISTY BARRITT

RIVER HEIGHTS

The case of the stunt double and a confused bad guy. Or something.

CHAPTER ONE

"EVERYONE IS JUST GOING to die when they see you!" Dizzy squealed and twirled me around in a makeup chair in my bathroom. "Can we say va-va-voom?"

She did a little chest circle and rolled her tongue in a catlike growl.

I glanced in the mirror and . . . I almost died myself.

Dizzy—a beautician and my aunt by marriage—had volunteered to do my makeup for a movie premiere and charity fundraiser I was about to attend. And she'd copied her trademark bright-blue eyeshadow—worn thick all the way up to the eyebrows—on me.

I looked like a clown. Or like someone the cast of *Mean Girls* had pranked.

But one look at Dizzy's hopeful expression, and I knew this was no prank. *She* thought I looked great. *I* thought there was no way I could face the public like this.

"It's . . . more than I could have ever expected," I said, my voice falsely cheerful. I had to utilize my acting skills in moments like these.

Dizzy beamed. She'd already said doing my makeup for

this event was the highlight of her year and that it made her feel famous. I couldn't burst her bubble.

The doorbell rang, and I sucked in a deep breath.

It was time.

I adjusted the adorable turquoise romper I was wearing. Yes, it was a romper, but it was a cute one. You had to see it to believe it. My stylist had given her thumbs-up, so it must be okay. Hollywood types like Miranda Worthington never got it wrong. Just look at those great outfits worn on exclusive catwalks at prestigious modeling shows.

Right?

I strode toward the front door and pulled it open. My heart skipped a beat when I saw Jackson Sullivan standing on the other side.

I swallowed hard, remembering with absolute clarity the last time he'd shown up at my door. We'd shared a passionate kiss that I was likely to never forget. Ever.

It wasn't unlike that smooch from *Spider-Man*, except no one was hanging upside down.

Speaking of which . . . Jackson and I still needed to talk about the aforementioned lip lock. We hadn't had time to, since I'd only arrived back from LA yesterday.

"Hey there." I sounded as self-conscious as Carrie at the prom right before the pig blood covered her.

I glanced Jackson over, soaking in his tux. His barely there beard. His intense green eyes, square jaw, and broad shoulders. Check, check, check, and check.

He rested one hand in his pocket, looking all casual and *GQ*-like. That wasn't to mention that he had the laid-back confidence of someone who couldn't care less what people thought of him.

That only made him so much more appealing.

He let out a low whistle. "You look gorgeous, Joey."

My cheeks heated. It didn't matter how famous I was. Sometimes I still felt like the girl with braces who didn't want to be called on in algebra class—mostly because I'd been daydreaming about boys and hadn't even heard the teacher's question.

Jackson's gaze stopped at my eyes, and he squinted.

The eyeshadow, I remembered.

It had to be the eyeshadow.

I offered a weak smile and shrugged. I'd explain my makeup later—when my dear aunt wasn't within earshot.

Jackson peered behind me. "Hey, Dizzy."

Actually, Dizzy being here was probably explanation enough.

Dizzy slipped past us, clutching her cosmetic bag like a medic on the battlefield. "Hey yourself. I was just leaving. I've got to get ready for the big premiere! The Hot Chicks and I will all be there, cheering you on. We had special shirts made saying, 'Joey Darling is my friend.' Don't you love that?"

"I do, and I can't wait to see you all," I said before exchanging another smile with Jackson.

My cheeks heated as our eyes met, and I remembered the very alluring feel of his lips against mine.

Which could never happen again.

Maybe *never* was a strong word. It could never happen again in the next . . . year, at least.

Okay, six months.

One month?

I really had to stick to my convictions. But it was so hard sometimes.

No sooner had Dizzy walked away than someone else trotted up my front steps and stopped with a bounce at the doorway. My neighbor and friend Zane Oakley stood there with a wide clueless grin.

I blinked. He was also wearing a tux—his was baby blue with suspenders and an obnoxious Hawaiian-themed bow tie. His tall, lean surfer bod was freshly scrubbed, but his wild, curly hair had a mind of its own. It defined Zane—free, natural, fun.

My stomach dropped and then squeezed as my gaze volleyed back and forth between both men.

What was Zane doing here? Did he think . . .

Oh no.

This was going to be more awkward than when Steve Harvey crowned the wrong woman as Miss Universe. And that had been *sooo* awkward.

Zane ignored Jackson and took my hand, twirling me around and letting out a low whistle. "Joey, my girl. You look sizzling hot."

I opened my mouth and then shut it again. Actually, right now I'd rather be Steve Harvey surrounded by scorned beauty queens than be caught between these two men who were vying for my affections. I hated the thought of hurting either of them.

"Thank you," I finally muttered, absently smoothing my romper and praying for a *Beam me up, Scotty* moment.

"You ready to go?" Zane looked at me and then glanced at Jackson, confusion stretching across his features. "You said the premiere started at six, so I figured you'd want to leave about now. Then I saw the limo pull up."

I nibbled on my bottom lip, trying to figure out how to break this to him. I could see where he might assume he'd be my date tonight since he had been my date in LA for that premiere.

Have I mentioned how messy my life was? One flub and hiccup after another, it seemed sometimes.

"I'm so sorry, Zane," I finally said. "I thought you knew. As a part of the premiere here, Jackson and I are going together. We're doing the whole hashtag: NHPDBlues thing, at the request of the mayor."

Jackson and I had been doing a bit of a Castle and Beckett thing. I "helped" him in his investigations—okay, not even!—and in return I got to hang out with him while on duty. The payoff? I'd developed a hashtag where I tweeted about the city and positive things happening here. Since I had more than four million Twitter followers, it seemed like a good trade-off.

I had secret motives, unfortunately.

My father had disappeared several months ago, and I was using the mayor's willingness to both appease and exploit me to try and find out information on my father. In the process, Jackson—a detective—and I had become friends.

It was a long, twisted tale. As were most of the tales in my life. My life made *The Brothers Karamazov* look simple.

Zane's mouth dropped open, and he took a step back looking . . . rejected. "Oh, I get it. I just assumed . . ."

My insides churned with unease . . . guilt . . . maybe some leftover bean dip.

I had to make this better.

"You could . . ." *Could what, Joey?* "You could . . . both ride with me."

What had I just said? That was the worst idea ever.

Certainly Zane would reject the suggestion, and everything would go on as scheduled. Then the two of us could talk later, and I could try to smooth things over.

"I don't want to intrude," Zane said.

"Oh, there's plenty of room in the limo," Jackson said, his gaze smoldering on mine. Something unspoken lingered in his eyes, but I had no idea what. It didn't appear to be irritation, but I just couldn't read him.

Dear me.

I opened my mouth to say something, to make things right, but no words would escape.

This idea sounded totally awful.

"That sounds totally fun," Zane said.

About as much fun as trying to climb out between a rock and a hard place. Or being the guy in *127 Hours* who had to amputate his own arm.

"Yes, fun." My voice sounded tight. Making things more awkward, I decided to clap with what I hoped looked like enthusiasm but more likely made me look like a cheerleading reject. "Okay, let's go then, before we're late."

My muscles pulled taut in an internal game of tug-of-war. Zane walked on one side of me and Jackson on the other down the little path toward the driveway. A limo had been waiting for fifteen minutes.

This wasn't uncomfortable. Not at all.

I mentally sighed.

Only me. This would happen only to me. I didn't suppose Jackson and I would be able to talk about that kiss on the drive after all. Nor would Zane and I be able to talk about our trip to LA. I suppose we could have on the plane ride back here, but why talk today about something I could put off until tomorrow?

And this was why I had problems.

Silenced stretched after we climbed into the limo. We all sat on the back bench, me in the middle.

As the AC blared and gentle music rolled from the

speakers, I straightened the hem of my romper and then cleared my throat.

I needed to talk about something safe—like the premiere tonight. It was a fundraiser for the children's wing at a local hospital. Doing something I loved and raising money for a good cause at the same time? How could you go wrong with those two things?

My movie *Family Secrets* had just released to popular and critical success. Then this opportunity had popped up, organized by the hospital fundraising team in conjunction with the mayor of Nags Head—he was one of my biggest fans. Then my manager, Rutherford, had gotten involved, wanting to bring some Hollywood to the Outer Banks. It had turned into something much larger than I'd ever imagined.

Now my movie, which officially released last weekend, would premiere locally on the lawn in an outdoor festival area that scooted up to the Albemarle Sound. People would bring beach chairs. Vendors would sell snacks—hopefully some fish tacos, because I needed to talk someone into buying me one. There would be a question-and-answer session, as well as a meet and greet afterward.

Win. Win. Win.

"Apparently, this event tonight has been the buzz of the town," Zane said. "I mean, look at all this traffic."

Croatan Highway—the main artery through town—was jam packed, looking more crowded than it did on Saturdays when one set of vacationing guests checked out and a new set rolled in. That was what I'd been forewarned about, at least. The height of tourist season was still a few weeks away.

"So here's a little secret that no one else knows," I said, not daring to look at either Jackson or Zane. Nope, straight ahead was a much safer bet. "Well, no one but a handful of people who are working this event. Can you keep it quiet until the show starts?"

Of course Jackson could. It was Zane I was worried about.

I plowed on ahead, not bothering to wait for their answers. "So, for starters, Carli Moreno will be there tonight."

"Who?" Jackson asked.

"She's my stunt double," I explained.

"Carli Moreno?" Zane's voice clearly showed he was impressed. "That's so cool. The two of you look so much alike that it's uncanny."

"We have a special opening planned," I said. "It was Carli's idea, and she flew all the way out here just to help me with it. I can't wait for you guys to see it."

"I look forward to it," Jackson said.

A few minutes later, the limo stopped at our destination. It was May, and the weather was perfect for this event. The sun was just beginning to set behind the stage area. Tons of cars were already here. Like, tons.

I'd heard they sold out at one thousand tickets.

Just like Mayor Allen hoped, this could do great things for the area. I already thought the Outer Banks had a lot of great things going for it. Thousands of tourists flocked here. Businesses were thriving. National magazines had featured the area on top-ten lists. But I supposed one could never get enough positive publicity, so here I was, being a dutiful citizen.

The chauffeur reached for my door.

"Here goes nothing," I muttered.

"You'll do great," Jackson softly murmured.

He always had a way of calming me down . . . unless I

was doing something stupid like interfering with a police investigation. Then he just got me fired up.

I took a deep breath before stepping out. As soon as I did, flashes began going off around me. Part press, part paparazzi. I was sure the *National Instigator* had their bloodthirsty vultures somewhere in the crowd.

For some reason, that tabloid really, really liked me. And when I say liked, I meant hated. It was a fine line when it came to these guys.

I looked over and realized that Jackson was flanking one side of me and Zane the other.

The press was going to *love* this. I shoved aside any thoughts on what the headlines might read. *Joey Darling Love Triangle? Joey Darling, Queen of Indecisiveness. Joey Darling, the Woman Who Couldn't Make Up Her Mind.*

The crowds cheered around me. Several thrust papers and pens forward for autographs. One person wore a paper mask with my face on it.

I supposed it was flattering . . . in a very strange way.

I sucked in a breath. This was a whole new level of stardom. I mean, I'd always had some die-hard fans. People often recognized me. Tabloids featured me.

But having a hit movie took this to a new level. I'd thought my career was dying faster than clean romantic comedies on the big screen. And the pace this all had happened took my breath away. Made me elated and overwhelmed at the same time.

Speaking of which . . . my head was beginning to spin.

I started to reach for someone's arm to steady me, but I couldn't decide whose I should take. Definitely not both Zane's and Jackson's.

So I decided to go solo and take neither to keep things simple.

They escorted me behind the stage area, which had been set up with a fake movie screen at the front and real curtains at the side. There was also an RV—or trailer— where I could wait or freshen up when needed.

I passed a security guard and approved Zane and Jackson to also go back. It wasn't until I was out of sight from the crowds and press that I released my breath. Now it was almost show time.

Almost.

Rutherford left the stagehands he was talking to and rushed toward me with an electronic tablet in his hands.

Rutherford James Seamore II had dark wavy hair that he wore slicked back. His face was pock marked from acne when he was younger. But he was one of the best managers in the business. The fact that he'd wanted to come out and help with this event was slightly suspect. However, he'd begun his illustrious career as a producer for the big award shows, so he knew how to handle a backstage.

"You ready for this?" Rutherford frowned. "And please remove that blue eyeshadow."

The eyeshadow! Gulp. I'd forgotten about it.

"It's worse than awful. In fact, it's hurting my eyes." He squinted as if I was blinding him.

Maybe he should be an actor. He was pretty good with dramatics.

Using my fingers, I wiped at it. I'd need to disappear into my trailer to fix it before I went onstage.

"The police chief wants me to check out something out front. Are you good?" Jackson asked, leaning close.

I nodded. "This area is very secure. I should be fine. Besides, I have . . . Zane?"

Where had he gone? I finally spotted him talking to one of the crew members.

"I'll be fine," I said anyway.

Jackson looked at me one more minute before leaving—somewhat reluctantly.

"Everything should be good to go," Rutherford said. "No one is going to forget this opening."

"I hope not."

"Alright, Carli is waiting to talk to you." He glanced at his watch. "We only have ten minutes until this shindig starts. Don't forget the eyeshadow."

"I won't," I called.

I rolled my eyes as I left him and made my way toward Carli, who was already harnessed up and waiting behind the screen. She'd climb some scaffolding and make her descent, busting through the fake movie screen.

My character in *Family Secrets* had done the same thing, and that scene was now a fan favorite. It was already being illegally recorded and plastered online everywhere. That was why I just knew people were going to love it.

"Joey!" Carli called, giving me a hug. "I can't wait for this."

"Me neither." I ran my eyes up and down. "Nice outfit."

Her romper looked just like mine. Her hair had been fixed just like mine. She even had the same shoes on. Not the same eyeshadow, however.

"We're twinsies!" She squealed like a Valley girl, though she was far from fitting that description. In fact, her parents were carnies, and she'd been an acrobat for a traveling show as a child.

"Thanks again for coming out here," I said.

"It's my pleasure. I've always wanted to come to the Outer Banks. Tim and I are going to make a mini vacay out of it. Got a house on the beach even."

"We'll have to get together before you leave then."

"I'd love to! We have to catch up. Especially since the start of my trip has been so horrible."

"Horrible? Why?" She had me curious now.

She glanced over my shoulder. "Rutherford is motioning that it's time for me to get in place. We'll have to talk later. Until then, we've got this, Joey."

I nodded, unsure why I felt nervous when she was the one in the harness.

"We've got this!" I echoed.

Carefully remaining out of sight, I watched as Carli climbed up on a platform and took her place. She gave me a thumbs-up, and I returned the gesture. Then I took some deep breaths. Stretched. Did the whole anxiety-reducing acts of pretending the audience was naked—which never worked. It only made me blush.

"Joey, get in place," Rutherford said. "It's about to begin."

I hadn't fixed my eyeshadow. I let out a sigh. I was going to have to live with it. Pretend it was on purpose. On trend. That I was making a statement.

"Got it." I walked to the side of the stage area and peered out from behind one of the curtains.

I spotted Dizzy and her friends, wearing their custom-made shirts. I spotted Jackson at the base of the stage, wearing his tux but looking like security. He always looked like security, and I secretly loved that. I wished my friend Phoebe could be here, but she'd taken a last-minute trip to Colorado to see one of her childhood friends.

Mayor Allen—a short man with a bald head and a lisp—walked onstage and introduced everyone to the event. The crowds cheered. My heart raced with healthy anticipation.

Right on cue, the fog machine started, and smoke filled the stage area.

Action-packed theme music began playing.

On the count of three, Carli jumped from the platform, hanging on a rope. She burst through the fake movie screen.

As she did, the crowds roared.

I rushed onto the stage, staying low so the fog would conceal me.

Carli would land. Disengage her harness. Then I'd take her place and wave to the crowd. It would be an entrance people would never forget.

Easy peasy, right? Showmanship at its finest. We'd be making people feel like they were getting their money's worth by coming here and supporting this charity.

As I rushed toward the designated spot, I tripped on . . . something.

I waved the fog out of my way, trying to see what had been left on the stage area.

But what I saw stopped me cold.

It was Carli. She was lying in a broken heap on the stage floor.

CHAPTER TWO

I KNELT BESIDE CARLI, trying to comprehend the situation. The crowds were cheering too loudly, the fog was too thick, and the moment seemed too surreal.

But this was real, and I had to do something. Every moment counted right now.

"Help!" I yelled, hoping someone would hear me over the music and noise.

People scrambled nearby, so someone must have heard something. I prayed they'd get here soon. Hadn't there been some paramedics stationed somewhere close?

I started to touch Carli, to reach for her, but I stopped myself. I didn't want to hurt her more. Her bones and body were twisted. Unnatural. Painful looking.

"Carli," I whispered. How had this happened?

At her name, her eyelids fluttered.

She was still alive. Alive!

A new surge of hope rushed through me.

I leaned closer. "Are you okay?"

"My harness . . ." she whispered, her voice scratchy and

strained. Her eyes looked dazed and slightly vacant. "The line . . . it . . . it was . . . cut."

As the fog began clearing, I glanced down at the ropes that had been around her midsection, and gasped. Sure enough, one of them had broken. But the ends weren't frayed. The cut looked clean. Purposeful.

My blood went ice cold.

"I can't . . . feel . . . my legs," Carli muttered.

My stomach dropped. No, no, no . . . But I could tell from the position in which she'd landed that this was bad. Really bad.

"What happened?" Jackson appeared beside me. His eyes widened when he spotted Carli. "Oh, dear Lord."

I knew he'd muttered it as a prayer. A gut-wrenching one at that.

He pulled out his phone, no doubt calling for more help.

Rutherford joined us, followed by Mayor Allen, Zane, and Carli's husband, Tim.

The curtains had been closed across the stage area to block the public from witnessing any more of the scene. I could already hear the murmur from the crowds though. They knew something was wrong. I prayed they hadn't seen too much.

This moment—Carli—shouldn't be exploited like this.

Everything was a blur around me.

Jackson knelt in front of Carli, talking to her, keeping her lucid.

Zane slipped an arm around my waist, probably in case I passed out.

Rutherford got on his phone, undoubtedly trying to get a head start on the PR of a disaster like this.

I still couldn't believe this had happened. I slapped my hand over my mouth, trying to look away but unable to do so.

Paramedics arrived quickly and huddled around her, stretcher in place.

Someone had stepped onto the other side of the curtain to give an update and ask everyone to remain calm.

"Zane, get Joey out of here," Jackson barked. "Don't take your eyes off her."

Don't take his eyes off me? What did that mean? It almost sounded like Jackson thought I was in danger also.

That was ridiculous. This was all a terrible accident.

Except Carli's harness had been cut.

My blood went even colder than the actors on the set of *Dr. Zhivago.*

"But—" I started.

"We'll talk later," Jackson said.

Zane ushered me backstage. My head spun as I tried to process everything. But I couldn't. Reality refused to set in. It was too big for me to comprehend right now.

"What's going on, Zane?" I asked, wishing he wasn't walking so fast that everything was a blur around me.

"I have no idea." He didn't stop walking until we were well out of sight from the crowds. Then he turned me to face him, and he looked just as confused as I was.

Before I could ask more questions, Jackson appeared. He wasn't walking all casual-like. No, he was on a mission, and each of his steps was urgent.

"We need to get you out of here," he said, taking my arm.

The concern on his face startled me on an entirely different level.

"Why? What's going on?" I asked.

"I'll explain later."

I dug my heels in, not liking this. "No, I need to know. Now."

"Joey . . ."

"I should stay here," I said, trying to compute the implications of this. "I need to explain to people what happened—"

"Someone just called in a bomb threat," Jackson said. "This whole festival park needs to be evacuated."

———

Everything around me stopped, and I felt as if I was in an alternate universe for a minute.

"A bomb threat?" I repeated.

Jackson nodded. "That's why we need to get you out of here."

I crossed my arms. "I'm not leaving."

"Don't be ridiculous."

"I'm not being ridiculous. I'm not leaving. People are here because of me. They need to be cleared out first."

"Joey . . ."

"I'm serious, Jackson. If I get out of here in one piece and someone else suffers, I'll never forgive myself. Besides, I'm no more important than anyone else here. I'll be okay."

He stared at me another moment, and I could see his wheels turning. Finally, he nodded.

"Go stay in the trailer until we clear the area. Understand?"

I nodded. "Got it."

Zane led me to the RV parked at the back of the property. I sat on the stiff brown couch inside, my head still spinning. Zane sat across from me, and it appeared his head was spinning also.

Neither of us said anything for a minute, but I could hear the rumble of vehicles outside. The evacuation was in progress. I only prayed it was in time. Or that the threat had been an empty one.

An empty threat would be annoying, frustrating, maddening—but better than someone getting hurt.

"I wonder how Carli is," I finally said, picturing her mangled body.

"She talked to you, right? That's a good sign." He seemed all laid back and surfer-like, but in a past life he'd been in sports medicine. Maybe he knew more than I often remembered to give him credit for.

"Zane, she said her harness line had been cut."

His eyes widened. "You mean, like, on purpose?"

I nodded. "That's exactly what I mean."

"Why would someone do that?"

"Why would someone make a bomb threat?" I leaned back into the couch again, wishing my head would stop spinning. But it didn't.

"This is all craziness." He rubbed his forehead. "Do you think it ties in with your super-stalker fan club?"

I released a sigh at the mention of that group. "I can't imagine they would take it this far. This isn't their MO."

"You're right. They like to taunt you, not ruin you."

My mind ran through everything that had happened since I arrived here at the park. There were so few people who were allowed backstage access. Each one's name was on a list, and a security guard was stationed at the entrance. There was a temporary fence up around that area even.

"Did you see anything, Zane?" I asked.

His eyes popped up to meet mine. "What do you mean?"

"You were talking to that member of the stage crew."

"Gerrard?"

I shrugged. "I don't know his name. But did you see anyone up in the scaffolding? Anyone acting suspicious?"

He shook his head. "No. But honestly, I wasn't looking either. I can talk to Gerrard. He's a part of the light crew, and he caught one of the most epic waves I've ever seen last year while we were down in Hatteras."

"We need to focus, Zane."

His face went back to serious in 5.2. "Of course."

"What do you see out there?" I asked.

Shoving the curtain aside, he peered out the window. "Everyone appears to be orderly. That's really all I can tell."

"Poor Carli . . ." She was all I could think about.

Her body . . . it looked bad. What if she could never do stunts again? What if she could never walk again, for that matter?

I squeezed my eyes shut.

When I opened them again, Zane was sitting beside me. His hands went to my shoulders, and he gently worked my muscles.

"It's going to be okay," he muttered.

I normally tried to refuse his massages—because massages led to other things. Kissing-like things. Things I needed to stay far away from.

But I didn't turn him down this time. No, my muscles needed some relief. And his warm hands felt so good against my skin.

I peeked my eyes open and drew in a deep, calming breath.

And that was when I saw it.

I raised a finger like ET phoning home.

But I wasn't phoning home.

I was pointing to a backpack. One I'd never seen before. One that wasn't supposed to be in this trailer.

And one that had a red blinking light shining through the canvas.

CHAPTER THREE

MY MUSCLES TENSED FASTER than those cars in *The Fast and the Furious*.

"We've got to get out of here," I muttered.

"Uh . . . yeah. I'd say so." Zane's eyes were fixated on the bag, and he appeared frozen.

I tried to swallow but second-guessed that movement also. "We should move carefully. Very carefully."

"Also agree."

I felt as stiff as a board as I stood. Zane followed my lead, and together we scooted around the bag, shuffling our feet. I remained intensely aware of every time the trailer swayed at my steps. The exit was only three feet away. I could do this. I just couldn't make any unexpected moves.

I was almost in the clear.

Until the door flew open.

I screamed. And I jumped. And then I froze, staring at the backpack and waiting for an explosion.

"What in the world are you doing, Joey?" Jackson stood in the door. He'd abandoned his bow tie and his jacket in favor of rolling up the white sleeves of his shirt.

And he looked good.

If only I had time to admire just how good. But I didn't.

I pointed at the bag, breathless with anticipation. "That."

I held my breath, hoping my sudden movement hadn't set anything off. It wasn't too late. At any time, an explosion could rip through the air and decide my very undecided future for me.

Jackson's eyes zeroed in on the ratty green book bag with the red light peeking through. "This was supposed to be a secure area," he muttered, an edge of contempt in his voice. "You two, get out of here. Now."

I had a feeling that meant Jackson was staying, and I was about to argue.

Before I could, Jackson grabbed me and flung me out of the trailer so fast that my feet could barely keep up. Zane followed behind me, no flinging involved.

But not Jackson, as expected. Sure, he'd stepped out, but he was already on his phone. Police cars, which had been stationed at the stage area, were already speeding this way. Another crew with barking dogs ran across the grass. Bomb-sniffing dogs, no doubt.

Zane and I darted away from the RV, not stopping until we reached the festival area. Lawn chairs had been left behind. Programs blew with the breeze. Food trucks had been abandoned.

I wondered if there were any fish tacos inside those trucks . . .

Focus, Joey. Focus.

I stared at the torn screen, a sad reminder of how things had gone wrong. A lone seagull cried overhead, and the air felt unusually heavy.

As I remembered the bomb, my heart slammed into my

rib cage, and I could hardly get enough breath to fill my lungs. I'd been sitting . . . by a bomb.

And I'd had no clue.

My gaze was fixed in the distance. On Jackson. The sunset smeared behind him in a pink-and-orange blur. The scene created a deceitfully peaceful backdrop to the urgent events of the evening.

What if that bomb exploded while Jackson was standing there? We'd never even talked about our kiss. And that kiss deserved to be talked about. Discussed. Dissected. Possibly repeated.

In a year or so, of course.

Zane's arm slipped around me, and he rubbed my bicep, glancing over his shoulder. "Everyone's gone and safe. That's the good news."

"That is good." Except . . . Carli wasn't safe.

I couldn't pull my thoughts from her. I pictured what she was probably going through right now. Diagnoses. Surgery. Averted plans.

Tears pressed at my eyes.

This was all horrible. So horrible.

And tonight was supposed to be so much fun.

And what about all the money we were supposed to be raising for the children's wing? What would happen to that? It could have done so much good.

I watched. I waited. I even prayed.

Finally, Jackson strode back over toward me and Zane.

"It's been diffused," he announced, his gaze flickering from me to Zane and back to me again.

"You mean, it was a real bomb?" I asked.

Part of me had expected it just to be a misunderstanding. I mean, who would leave a bomb in my trailer? That was just ridiculous. It was probably a radio. Or toy. Or something else easily confusable. Which was usually just about everything for me.

"It was a real bomb," Jackson said, his hands going to his hips. He seriously reminded me of James Bond right now in that partly removed tux. "And it was only five minutes from going off."

The blood drained from my face as he finished his sentence. "But . . ."

I tried to let the implications of that sink in. Jackson said nothing, only nodded.

"You don't have to worry anymore," he said. "It's not going to hurt anyone."

"That's . . . that's good." Because one person was too many. Carli was too many. Why did trouble continually follow me like a lost puppy dog needing a home?

"Listen, why don't you stick around a few more minutes, and then I'll drive you to the hospital," Jackson said. "I'm assuming you want to go there and check on your friend."

"I can drive her," Zane said.

Jackson's jaw twitched. "Do you have a car here?"

Zane frowned. "No, I guess I don't."

"Then just hang out a few minutes. I need to wrap this up, and then I'll take you there. I have to head that way anyway."

He hurried back over to the law-enforcement gathering in the distance. As he did, I heard a car rumbling across the gravel driveway leading to the festival area. I watched as an expensive-looking SUV pulled up in the lane beside us.

Maybe the occupants hadn't gotten the memo that this event was canceled. A disaster. A total blowout.

The vehicle stopped, and someone hopped out. Paused. Looked around. Squinted with confusion.

My bad day had just gotten a thousand times worse.

Because my ex, Eric Lauderdale, had just arrived.

Eric, my abusive ex-husband, who'd been cast with a cameo in *Family Secrets*.

He'd been a Calvin Klein model before becoming an actor. He'd gone on to play Captain Gorgeous, a role that people still mocked him for and that had spurred uncountable spoofs. Right now he looked so ridiculously Hollywood with his aviator glasses, unbuttoned shirt, and beard. Didn't he know that beards were cesspools of germs—that they were dirtier than toilets?

He saw me, and a satisfied grin crossed his face.

I knew exactly what he was thinking. He was smirking because my event was ruined. Or he thought no one had shown up. Either would be a win for Eric. Anything that made me look bad.

He strode toward me.

"Is that . . ." Zane whispered.

I scowled. "Yep."

"Oh no . . ." Zane muttered, as if he knew what was about to play out.

He'd met Eric briefly in LA. Zane knew I tried to avoid the man at all costs, but there was no avoiding him now. We were like two people in the Wild West about to face off— only without guns. Insults were our weapons of choice.

"What are you doing here?" I barked as soon as Eric was close enough to see my displeasure.

"My plane was late, so I just arrived here." He nudged his sunglasses down. It was a good thing since . . . oh, I didn't know . . . it was getting *dark* outside.

My eyes drifted beside him. Of course his new girlfriend, Tiffany, was here. She scrambled to catch up with him and now flanked him like a life-sized blow-up Barbie.

Inflated described her in so many ways. Artificial body parts. Air-filled brain. Ego.

No, that's not nice, Joey. Maybe she's perfectly decent.

"Nice eyeshadow," she muttered with a sneer.

Okay, she wasn't nice at all.

"Your plane being late doesn't explain what you're doing here," I said again.

Eric scowled. "Rutherford asked me to come out for the event. He didn't tell you?"

Rutherford did this? That confirmed it. I hated Rutherford. Absolutely hated him for putting PR before my emotional well-being. I was going to write my own *10 Things I Hate about You* movie, and Rutherford would be the star.

"Joey," Zane whispered, his breath tickling my cheek.

I'd nearly forgotten he was beside me. "Yes?"

He gave me a warning look, as if he was anticipating my claws coming out. He would have been right. Something about Eric brought out the worst side of me, a side I didn't like.

"Why in the world would Rutherford want you to be here?" I finally said.

"To help promote my new book, I suppose."

"The one where you talk about—and exaggerate—our relationship in detail?" I nearly screeched.

I'd heard rumors about some of the things he was going to say about me within those pages. They weren't kind. Apparently, he'd presented me as a demon and himself as an angel. I was Loki; he was an Avenger. I was Gargamel; he was an innocent Smurf.

"Yep, that's the one." He glanced around. "But this event looks like a real dud. Waste of a plane ticket, I guess. At least we'll get to see the area."

I balled my hands into fists, seriously thinking about punching his smug little face.

Just then, Jackson appeared.

He didn't even acknowledge Eric. No, he took my arm and led me away. "We need to get you to the hospital."

I didn't look back either. I needed to get out of here before I did something I regretted.

But the next time I saw Rutherford, I would give him a piece of my mind for asking Eric to come here.

CHAPTER FOUR

THE NEXT THING I KNEW, I was in the back of a police sedan. Apparently, another officer had let Jackson have his car. Zane scooted in beside me, and Jackson climbed in the front seat.

We drove away from the area, leaving Eric and Tiffany standing in the darkness.

I tried to control my breathing. Control my racing heart and out-of-control adrenaline.

Did you ever see that movie *Sleeping with the Enemy*? Yeah, that could describe my marriage with Eric—toxic.

How badly I wished I could forget that time in my life. That I could undo my mistakes. But life didn't work that way. So we moved on and imagined that voodoo dolls were real and hoped karma really happened.

Eric had started off as my dream man—my first love—but as his layers had been peeled away, I'd discovered an abuser. Someone who put me down, who felt threatened by my successes, who reminded me daily that I wasn't good enough in any area of my life. That had quickly morphed into fits of anger, where he'd thrown things. Where he'd cornered me. Where he'd tried to choke me.

But my eye-opening moment came when he pushed me down the stairs at our house, took my phone, and left me for dead. I'd driven myself to the hospital, but I'd wrecked on the way there, and doctors had assumed my injuries were related to the crash.

Only Jackson and my best friend, Starla, knew the truth.

Throughout it all, Eric maintained a charming facade, allowing people to think he was the kindest, most polite person in Hollywood. I could hardly stomach the thought.

As I drew in another deep breath, I looked up. I saw Jackson glancing at me in the rearview mirror, silently evaluating my emotional state. When Zane squeezed my knee, I looked away.

"Any clues as to who that backpack belonged to?" I finally asked, the first to break the silence.

"There were no indications," Jackson said.

"So someone called in the bomb threat," I said, making a mental timeline, "after Carli was injured."

"That's correct. He wanted us to evacuate the premises."

"It had to be the same person who tampered with Carli's harness . . ." Now I was thinking like Raven Remington, the TV character who'd made me famous. She was the smartest person I didn't know. And that would be because she wasn't real.

"There's a good chance," Jackson said.

"So it had to be someone who had backstage access," I continued, thinking aloud.

"That's our first assumption. My guys are questioning everyone now."

I leaned back, happy to focus on the facts instead of my emotional turmoil. "The security guard should have a log of everyone who came and went. He should have been stationed there from before the rehearsal until the start of the show."

"That's my understanding as well," Jackson said. "We're taking this very seriously."

I leaned back, still processing. "I just can't figure out why anyone would do this. It doesn't make sense. This was for a children's wing. I mean, who was the target here? The hospital? Carli?"

"We're trying to figure this out," Jackson said. "It's still early, and we have a lot of people to question before we'll even begin to have any answers."

Think like Raven, Joey. What would the first step be? The best place to look for answers?

I snapped my fingers in a *bingo!* moment. "Did you trace the phone number yet?"

"It was a burner phone," Jackson said.

I let out a grunt. I should have known it wouldn't be that easy. "How about prints? Were there any left on the bag?"

"My guys are looking into it."

Before I could ask any more questions, we pulled up to the hospital. I couldn't wait to hear an update on Carli.

———

The hospital was a circus of a whole 'nother sort.

When I arrived with Jackson and Zane, the press had already shown up. They were parked outside, and hospital security appeared to be talking to them and explaining whether or not they were welcome here.

Hopefully, they were telling them to go away.

Anxiety rushed through me as I bypassed the headline mongers and stepped into the building. Jackson flanked one side of me, and Zane the other.

As soon as I started down the hallway, my stomach churned with bad memories. There was almost a sort of PTSD that came over me as I remembered being here after my car crash. Just the smell of antiseptic made me want to throw up.

We took the elevator up to a third-floor waiting room. I paused outside the area and glanced through the glass door leading into the space.

I recognized a few faces. The mayor was already there, as well as Tim. I also spotted a few people from the production, including the technical manager and the guy Zane had been talking to.

Most looked stunned. Some people's shoulders stooped as they bent over in their seats, their heads lowered, as if praying. The mood was somber, to say the least.

I knew that Jackson would eventually question each of them. Normally, I'd try to be right at his side, listening—or eavesdropping—on every word. But this time I was in too much shock.

My gaze focused on Tim, who was in the corner by himself. I needed to talk to him—for more than one reason.

"Would you excuse me a minute?" I said to Zane and Jackson.

"Of course," Jackson said.

"I'm going to grab something to drink at the vending machines," Zane said.

"I need to talk with the chief." Jackson nodded toward the man who was striding down the hallway toward us.

As I pushed through the glass doors and walked toward

Tim, my palms felt sweaty, reminding me I was nervous. Gently, I lowered myself onto the gray pleather seat beside him. I didn't feel like I was walking on eggshells. No, I felt like I was sitting on them.

He glanced up at me, his eyes bloodshot and red. "Thanks for coming, Joey."

I squeezed his knee. "Of course."

I'd hung out with Tim and Carli before in LA. I didn't know him really well, but he'd always seemed like a cool guy. And I knew Carli was head over heels in love with him. They'd been married a couple of years, which was like decades in Hollywood.

"She's in surgery."

"Did the doctors say anything about her injuries?" My throat felt dry and hoarse with each word. I hoped for the best but tried to prepare myself for the worst.

"I heard that she may have a broken back."

He glanced over at me again, the depth of pain in his eyes making me reel.

"What happened out there, Joey?"

I shook my head. I'd replayed the event over and over in my mind, but nothing had changed. I hadn't remembered anything new or startling. "I have no idea, Tim. Everything went fine in rehearsal earlier. You saw it yourself. You were there."

He nodded and wiped a hand over his face. "I know. I just don't understand. Carli is careful. She doesn't let stuff like this happen. I mean, she's done some intense stunts. Stunts I didn't want her to do. I didn't think anything about this one though. It seemed pretty run of the mill."

"I agree. If I thought I was putting her at risk by doing this, I would have changed our game plan. No one foresaw this happening."

"What am I going to do?" He hung his head and rested it in the crook of his hand.

I rubbed his back, wishing I could magically think of words that would make this all better. But there was nothing I could say. This was a tragedy, and I was praying for the best possible outcome. But I knew how grim this seemed.

"She's a fighter," I finally said. "She talked to me onstage, you know. She was lucid. That has to be a good sign."

He jerked his head back in surprise, and his eyes burned into mine. "What did she say?"

That was when I remembered the painful truth about what had happened. Should I tell him what Carli had revealed? Did he already know that this might not have been an accident? Panic started to envelop me.

"She . . ." I stopped myself and sighed. I couldn't keep this information from him. I wouldn't do that. "She said she thought the line was tampered with."

He let out a groan and dropped his head again. The next instant, he sprang to life and punched the wooden table in front of us, letting out a gut-wrenching moan. Magazines jumped off the table, and everyone in the room jolted from their chairs.

"I'm so sorry, Tim. The police are on this. They're going to figure out what's going on."

He said nothing. And there was nothing more I could say either. So I sat with him for a few more minutes.

A noise caught my ear, and I lifted my head. The TV in the corner was playing the news.

A breaking-news anchor announced that actress Joey Darling had been critically injured during a movie release event in Nags Head, North Carolina.

I sucked in a quick breath. Of course people had thought Carli was me. That was the way we'd planned it.

That thought caused a Titanic-sized lump to sink in my stomach.

"Joey?" Tim said.

"Yes?"

"You've got to figure out how this happened. Please."

How could I say no? "Of course. I'll do whatever I can."

CHAPTER FIVE

———————

I DIDN'T KNOW what else to do but sit with Tim. So that was what I did.

Neither of us had anything to say, and that was okay. Instead, I thought and prayed and watched people.

Eventually my thoughts stopped at this: If that line had been purposefully cut, then who had done it?

I glanced at the people in the waiting room. A few weren't with this incident but, from what I'd overheard, had a friend in a car accident. The rest were the technical crew, but they'd been hired locally and hadn't known Carli until today.

Who else had been backstage? The technical director had been in charge of playing the movie and setting up the screen. Zane's friend had been a stagehand—he'd moved microphones and helped with lights. There had been a security guard who kept an eye on the backstage area. I wasn't sure, but I thought he was a local guy.

Then there was Tim, who'd also acted as the stunt coordinator. And, of course, there'd been Rutherford, the mayor, Zane, Jackson, and me.

Was someone on that list guilty?

My other question was this: What had happened between the rehearsal and the actual show? The security guard should have stayed at the back of the stage area. No one unauthorized should have been able to come or go.

I continued to think it through, trying to figure out if I'd missed anything. Later, I'd see if I could find any videos of the event. Maybe someone had accidentally recorded something suspicious.

I let out a soft breath and sighed.

I didn't want to be an insensitive clod, but I did have a few questions to ask.

"Tim?"

He turned toward me. "Yeah?"

"When did you guys get into town?"

"Yesterday at six."

"What did you do after you arrived?" I asked.

"Grabbed a bite to eat and then went back to the house where we're staying."

"Did anything strange happen? I mean, if this was purposeful, I need to figure out who might be behind it. Who might have had a gripe with Carli?"

His face darkened. "Now that you mention it, we ran into an old friend of Carli's yesterday."

My spirits lifted. A lead! "Who's that?"

"Her name is Helena Briggs. She and Carli were on the carnie scene together up until six years ago when Carli became a stuntwoman."

"Helena happened to be in town?" I didn't really go for the whole coincidence thing. Not usually, at least. I went for it about as easily as I went for a role in a telenovela. Yeah, since I didn't speak Spanish, those were pretty much a no go.

"That's what she said. I thought it was weird. Apparently the two had a weird history also."

"What do you mean?"

"Helena hated Carli," he said. "When they were traveling with the carnie scene, Helena was always competing with Carli and trying to outdo her."

"How so?"

He shrugged. "I don't know. Carli would learn how to climb an aerial silk twenty feet in the air, and Helena would decide to go for thirty feet. Junk like that. Anyway, nothing seemed to have changed when we ran into her. She seemed pretty placid on the outside, but Carli said she saw that same competiveness in her eyes."

"Did you tell the police that when they questioned you? I assume they've talked to you already."

"Some detective did. Not your friend. And I didn't even think about mentioning it."

"Can I mention this to Jackson—Detective Sullivan?" I corrected myself.

"If you want," he said. "But I don't want to stir up any trouble for Carli."

"Why would that stir up trouble?"

"If I'm wrong and Helena catches wind that I started the rumor, she'll be furious. Apparently the carnie world is a small one. People don't take betrayal lightly—you become an outcast."

"Wow. I had no idea."

"Yeah, Helena could make Carli's life miserable. So please keep this on the down low."

"Will do."

Just then, a new person appeared at the door.

Rutherford.

———

I stormed over to Rutherford before he could push his way inside the room, grabbed his arm, and led him to a corner of the hallway, where I would try my best not to make a scene among the cast of *Grey's Anatomy*. I mean, the doctors and nurses.

"How could you?" I demanded with a seething hiss.

The hallway went quiet behind me.

Rutherford glanced over and tugged on his collar. "What are you talking about?"

"How could you invite Eric to this event? *My* event!"

"It's not abnormal for other cast members to show up." His gaze perused the crowd behind us again, and a reddish hue of heat rose from his neck to his cheeks.

"You know exactly what I'm talking about," I said through clenched teeth, trying desperately to keep my emotions under control.

"I think you're just a little upset right now, Joey." His tone clearly stated that he was trying to appease me. It was insulting.

"You know good and well what I'm talking about," I whispered. "This has nothing to do with Carli. You are an insensitive clod."

He pressed his lips together, mentally regrouping. I could read him like a book, and I didn't even read books.

"Joey, you know I represent Eric also."

My mood darkened even more. "You wanted to use this as a ploy to help him with book sales. Don't play stupid. This was all about making more money and getting more publicity. You were never in this for the children's wing."

"Of course I was." He, at least, made an effort to look offended.

I shook my head, not falling for this anymore, and took a step back. "No, you weren't. And, oh, by the way—you're fired."

He blinked. "You can't fire me."

"Of course I can."

He lowered his voice and glanced around once more, as if to make sure no one was watching. "I made you, Josephine Schermerhorn."

I almost gasped at his use of my real name. No one ever used that anymore. Most people couldn't even pronounce it. But I wasn't going to be deterred here—that was exactly what he was hoping for.

"You give yourself too much credit," I retorted.

"I can ruin you." His nostrils flared.

Oh, I was doing a great job of ruining myself. His threat didn't scare me. "I refuse to let someone work for me who thinks only about himself."

He narrowed his eyes. "You're going to regret this, Joey."

"I doubt that." No, what I regretted was ever hiring him in the first place.

————

Just as Rutherford stormed away, I leaned against the wall and tried to collect my thoughts.

If there was one thing I'd learned, it was that you had to strike while the iron was hot. If I wanted to figure out some answers, being here at the hospital might be one of the best times to do so. The most likely pool of suspects were all right here.

I glanced into the waiting room.

I wanted to start with Gerrard, partly because he was

Zane's friend. The man had dreadlocks and gave off a mellow, carefree surfing vibe. His skin was prematurely wrinkling—probably from hours in the sun—and his teeth were quite possibly nicotine stained.

He looked up when I approached him, and his eyes lit with curiosity.

"Can I talk to you?" I whispered.

"Yeah, sure."

I nodded toward the hallway, and he followed me there. I stood out of sight from the rest of the waiting-room occupants, trying to give this conversation some privacy.

"I loved *Family Secrets*, by the way." He shoved his hands in his pockets, looking halfway shy.

"Thank you. You and Zane know each other?"

He nodded. "Yeah, we go way back. I had to move up to Virginia to get a real job though. More opportunities up that way."

I shifted. "Look, my name is attached to this event, so I want to get to the bottom of what happened."

It wasn't so much that my name was attached as I just wanted answers, but I wasn't sure most people would understand that.

"I get that," he said.

This was a good starting point. "Were you at the festival venue between rehearsal and the actual performance?"

He nodded. "Yeah, yeah. Of course."

"What exactly was your job?"

"I was helping Jim—he runs the company. So I set up lights and the curtain. The fake movie screen. Don't worry —I signed a confidentially clause first."

"Did you see anything suspicious between rehearsal and the opening?" I continued.

He rubbed his chin and sighed. "I keep thinking about

it. Honestly, I was running around double-checking every-thing. People started to get there super early. Then I went over and bought a fish taco."

He got a fish taco and I didn't. Not fair.

"I didn't see anything," he concluded. "I wish I had."

"So there was no one suspicious backstage?" I mean, someone had done this. Somehow. Sometime.

He sighed and rubbed his chin again. "Here's who I remember being back there. Carli and her husband were eating out near the trailer. The mayor and that other guy—your manager maybe?—were on the sidelines discussing politics. Jim, who owns the company, was checking the projector to make sure everything would work."

That sounded right to me also.

"Someone would have had to climb up that scaffolding in order to mess with the harness," Gerrard continued. "I don't see how anyone could have done it without being spotted."

That was the problem—neither could I.

CHAPTER SIX

AFTER I THANKED Gerrard for his time, I talked to Jim, and he told me the same thing as Gerrard.

I couldn't see where Jim would have motive to do this. It had put the reputation of his company on the line, after all.

Finding answers was going to be harder than I thought. But I wasn't going to give up.

As I stood by the waiting room, I spotted Eric at the end of the hallway. He smiled, his fake white teeth gleaming, as he waved a charming hello to someone out of my sight.

You've got to be kidding me. Couldn't I catch a break?

Before I could pounce on Eric, Jackson stepped out of an alcove where the water fountain was. He'd probably been waiting for me. Did that mean he'd overheard my conversation with Rutherford?

Jackson grabbed my arm before I could do something else I regretted. My list of regrets was getting so long, and the night was only just beginning.

"You stay here," Jackson muttered, leaning close and using his no-nonsense voice. "I'll handle him."

I wanted to argue, but maybe it was better this way. I

was already drawing too much attention to myself when all the focus right now should be on Carli. Jackson could easily put Eric in his place. Someone needed to.

I finally nodded, giving Jackson permission to do his thing.

In the meantime, I needed to compose myself. Again.

I slipped into the women's bathroom and splashed some water on my face. As I came up, I saw that bright-blue eyeshadow and frowned. It was even worse than I'd remembered.

I grabbed a paper towel and began scrubbing it off. I wasn't sure what kind of makeup Dizzy had used, but it was some heavy-duty stuff. It took me six paper towels before I finally got most of the color off my lids.

At that point I'd pretty much scrubbed the rest of my makeup off also, so I looked . . . actually, I didn't look as bad as I expected. My early morning runs were doing me some good and adding some color back to my cheeks.

I wouldn't think about premature wrinkles and skin cancer. Not right now. I had bigger, more urgent fish to fry.

Besides, I didn't even bring my purse, so I couldn't touch up my makeup if I wanted.

I stepped back into the hallway, bracing myself to possibly see Eric.

Instead, I collided with Zane.

Running into people was the theme in my life today.

"There you are," he said. "I went to grab some of this vitamin-infused water, and when I got back, you were gone."

He'd tugged off his obnoxious bow tie and that pale-blue tux jacket. I had no idea where he'd left them, and I didn't care at the minute. My adrenaline was starting to crash, and my body wanted to crash with it.

Yes, I was exhausted after all the events and confrontations of the evening.

But I didn't want to leave this hospital until I knew more about Carli. I wouldn't sleep until I heard an update on how she was doing.

"Are you okay, Joey?" Zane asked, studying my face.

I sagged against the wall, ignoring all the antibiotic-resistant microbes that were probably lingering there, threatening to give me some kind of skin-eating bacteria. They were like those aliens from *The Host*, only on a microscopic level. "No, I'm not okay."

He reached for me, and I didn't resist. He wrapped his long, muscular arms around me and held me tight.

"Everything wasn't supposed to go like this," he muttered. "I know."

No, it wasn't. Today was supposed to be fun. A positive boost for the area. Maybe a morale boost for me, whose career had been dying up until a few weeks ago.

None of that really mattered. Not when a friend's life was on the line. That was the most important thing right now.

"Why do these things keep happening, Zane?" I mumbled into his chest, relishing the familiar scent of coconut and surfboard wax.

"I don't know, sweetie. I wish I did."

I pictured the crowd at the premiere. Their excitement as it turned to panic. Their expectation of entertainment as it morphed into the fear of real danger.

I could hardly stomach the thought of it.

"Have you heard any updates?" I asked, my throat dry, like my Central Worry Processing Center had sucked away every available amount of moisture in my body to fuel itself.

He stepped back—only a little. He still kept one arm

around me and pulled out his phone. "My friend Henry has been texting me—he was in the audience when everything happened. He said it was chaos after the police announced the evacuation, but everyone left the festival area in a pretty mature fashion."

"That's good news."

"The mayor told everyone that they'd receive an email as a follow-up on rescheduling the event."

"Rescheduling?" That was the first I'd heard of that.

Zane shrugged. "Just repeating what I heard."

I hung my head. I knew this wasn't my fault. Not exactly, at least. But it felt like a mess, and I was in the middle of it, so why not blame me? I was the headliner here, after all.

Jackson's shadow appeared beside me, and his face darkened when he saw Zane's arm around me. He kept it professional, though I could see his jaw twitch.

"Eric and his friend left," he announced.

"Left town?" One could only hope.

He shrugged. "I didn't go that far. I just told them they shouldn't be here. He argued for a few minutes but then left at his girlfriend's urging."

"Thank you." My voice cracked as I said the words.

Our gazes caught for a moment, and I could see something unspoken in Jackson's gaze.

The problem was, I didn't know what that unspoken thing was.

Before we could say—or not say—anything else, the doctor walked into the waiting room. His gaze found Tim, and he sat beside him.

I held my breath as I waited to see what happened.

I prayed Carli was okay, but I had a bad feeling about this.

CHAPTER SEVEN

————————————

AS SOON AS the doctor finished speaking, Tim hung his head. I couldn't see his face. Couldn't read his expression.

But his body language wasn't good.

When the doctor departed, I slipped into the waiting room. I sat beside Tim, not saying anything. He would talk when—and if—he needed to.

After a couple minutes, Tim looked up at me, his eyes even more bloodshot than before.

"She came through the surgery okay." He sucked in a long breath that was full of emotional turmoil. "Her leg is broken in two places, a rib is cracked, and one of her vertebra is fractured. There's swelling around it, which is what's causing her paralysis."

"Is it permanent?"

"They're not sure yet. She's still on a lot of morphine and really out of it."

"So the prognosis is . . ." I wanted to say *good*. I wanted to say that was what I'd understood from this conversation. But I wasn't sure what everything meant exactly.

"I don't know, Joey." He ran a hand over his face again. "I think it's going to be a long road ahead. But she's alive."

"That's right. We'll take this step by step."

He wiped his eyes before shaking his head. "This is just the first step in what could be a long journey though."

I squeezed his shoulder, desperate to do something to help him. "Are you going to try and get some sleep tonight?"

He shook his head. "Not tonight. I want to stay close."

"You have to take care of yourself also, you know."

He nodded. "I know. But when my dad died last year, Carli was there for me twenty-four seven. I'm not leaving her now."

I got that. "Let me know if you need anything. Can I get you a drink right now? Something to eat?"

"No, I'm good. But thank you, Joey. You're a real sweetheart, just like everyone says. Well, everyone but Eric. But don't worry—he'll get what's coming to him."

My lips twitched up in a half smile. "Thanks."

"I mean it."

———

I saw Jackson waiting for me in the hallway, and I figured something was up. I slipped out and met him.

"How is she?" Jackson asked.

"She came through the surgery okay, but it will be a while before the doctors know the extent of her injuries," I said.

"Well, it's a start." Jackson shifted, and I knew something else was up. "Joey, we need to ask you some questions. The hospital is going to let us use their conference room."

I'd figured the time would come when I'd have to get all

police official about this. "Yes, absolutely. I'd be happy to assist you."

"Assist me?" Jackson asked.

"In the investigation." I had to sell myself as someone who actually had these skills, even though I knew good and well I didn't.

Jackson let out an amused *hm-hm*.

I stepped past an officer who was set up outside the conference room door. Officer Windsor, also known as Officer I Like Duck Donuts.

The scent of artificial roses and mints surrounded me as the door closed behind me. Black-and-white beach pictures hung around the room like an art gallery. A pleasant coral color covered the walls. Paper, pencils, recorder, and cups of water were spread out on the table.

There was only one other person in here. Another detective. I thought his name was Gardner. Bill maybe?

I dropped onto a leather conference chair, feeling halfway numb inside and halfway painfully aware of everything around me.

Instead of both detectives sitting across from me like English soldiers facing off against William Wallace in *Braveheart*, Jackson sat beside me. He'd be my Robert the Bruce.

Wait, hadn't Robert the Bruce betrayed good old William? Or was that just in the movie?

I mentally sighed. It didn't matter.

"Joey." Jackson laced his fingers together and stared at me like a professional instead of a friend. "Detective Gardner will be heading this investigation. At this point, we're not sure who the intended target was in this crime."

The blood drained from my face. "What do you mean?"

"We mean that you and Carli looked and dressed alike.

For all intents and purposes, it was supposed to be you bursting through the movie screen. Only someone who was at rehearsal would have known for sure that it was Carli instead. Plus, that bomb was left in your trailer."

I could hardly find my words. "You really think that someone planned this, hoping to hurt me?"

"We think it's a possibility." Jackson's compassionate eyes met mine. "I'm sorry."

Cold fear pulsed through me. I was the target, possibly? Someone wanted to kill me . . . again? Why couldn't I catch a break here? Why would anyone hate me this much?

"Is there anyone who might want you dead, Joey?"

That was a loaded question. "You know everything that's happened since I moved here, Jackson."

He swallowed hard and kept his voice even and steady as he said, "I know, but I need to make this all official."

I crossed my arms, not really wanting to rehash all the bad things that had happened to me. But I understood what he was saying. "Sure thing. Let's see . . . there's my super-stalker fan club."

They were a group of unknown people who sent me clues about local mysteries and investigations, who watched my every move, and who were my biggest fans. They were trying to keep Raven Remington alive. And they were extreme, to say the least.

"Okay, who else?" Jackson asked.

I swallowed hard, remembering everything that had happened over the past few months. "There's also the unknown person or people who may be involved with my father's disappearance. We don't know who they are either."

"Okay."

I continued to think this through. Who else would want me dead? One other person's mugshot came into my mind.

If I said his name, I'd sound bitter. I said it anyway. "I suppose you could put Eric on that list."

Jackson blanched. "You think Eric is capable of doing something like this?"

My gaze locked on Jackson's. Jackson was one of the only people who knew the truth about what had happened between me and Eric. He knew that Eric had left me for dead. I knew he had to ask that question, but I really wished he hadn't.

"He can't stand it that my career is taking off and his isn't. That could be a motive," I finally said.

"He didn't arrive until after it was all over," Jackson said.

"That's what he said. He's a pathological liar, so I don't believe most of what comes from his lips." Yep, I sounded bitter.

Part of me thought I should use my acting skills to conceal any bad feelings. But as someone who got paid to pretend to be someone else, I'd learned that there was a lot to be said for authenticity.

Some people misunderstood or abused the idea of being real. They used it as an excuse to indulge in and justify all the ugly sides of themselves. I didn't want to be that person. But I did want to be honest and have integrity.

I sounded like my dad.

Jackson nodded slowly. "We'll double-check his flight times."

"And don't forget Rutherford." I was on a roll. I mean, how many people would have this many possibilities on who wanted them dead? I was so . . . special.

"He looked pretty angry earlier."

I scowled when I remembered that conversation. "He

was pretty angry. Anger can cause people to do horrible things."

However, he wasn't really angry with me until after the accident. I still didn't take his name back though. He was conniving. My dad said you showed integrity in the small, private things you did, not in the large, public displays.

In fact, maybe we should focus on being authentic with integrity. I thought my dad would approve of that. Maybe I could even do a PSA on the topic.

"Anyone else?" Jackson asked.

I remembered what Tim had told me about Helena. Should I mention her? I wasn't sure, so I didn't. I hoped I wasn't screwing things up.

I also remembered my conversations with Gerrard and Jim. But they hadn't offered me any new information, and I was certain the police had already talked to them as well.

"I'd say that's a good start. Honestly, I can't think of anyone else. Not right now, I can't. Give me enough time and . . ."

Jackson leaned toward me, his gaze all Christian Bale-intense-like. "How about Carli? You're good friends with her. Did she ever mention anything to you? Anyone she has problems with?"

I pressed my lips together in thought. "I just talked to her at rehearsal. Now that you mention it, she did seem upset about something, but she was going to tell me later. With everything that happened, I forgot about it."

"Joey, there's one other thing," he said.

"What's that?" I braced myself for whatever he had to say.

"I don't think you should be alone right now."

"Why not?" I knew the answer, but I asked anyway.

"Until we know who the true target was, we should use the utmost caution."

"So what are you suggesting?" I didn't even want to ask. Truly.

"I'm suggesting that you not be alone until we have more answers."

CHAPTER EIGHT

"ZANE, would you take Joey home and stay with her?" Jackson asked once we were out of the conference room and standing in the hallway. "We've arranged a special exit from the hospital so that no one sees her leave. One of the officers will drive you."

"Um . . . hello? I'm right here." I waved my hand.

"Of course I can do that," Zane said.

Jackson look at me finally. "I'll come by after I wrap things up here."

"I can keep an eye on her tonight." Zane leaned toward me, his chest puffing up ever so slightly. "It's no problem."

Jackson stared at him a minute, his eyes seeming to calculate his next step and waging if he could trust Zane or if he thought Zane would dump me at the first sign of a good surf. "Sure. Keep the doors locked. I'll keep an eye on her tomorrow."

"Don't I have any say in this?" I asked. "I mean, this is my life. Maybe I don't want anyone staying with me."

"Don't be ridiculous," Zane said.

"It's not an option," Jackson said.

I stared at them both, taking turns giving them dirty looks, which was much more challenging than it sounded.

"Until we know you're not in any danger, we need to be cautious," Jackson finally said.

"I agree," Zane said.

Oh great . . . *now* they wanted to work together? This was going to be cozy.

Usually the two men couldn't stand each other. Years ago, they'd fought over a girl, which had left some bad blood between them. Now they both had their sights set on me, and I had no idea what to do about it.

It was like the love triangle from *Sweet Home, Alabama* playing out in real life. It was one of the few movies where I didn't know which guy I wanted the girl to end up with because both were honest possibilities.

"I'll walk you to the exit, just to make sure everything is clear," Jackson said.

"Sure, why not?" Like it would do any good to argue when both their egos were displayed like peacock feathers for all to see.

No, I was better off just listening obediently. I'd have to choose my battles wisely, like Frodo in *Lord of the Rings*. Sci-fi fans loved it when I got all geeky on them. But now that I thought about it, I wasn't really sure Frodo ever had to choose his battles. I didn't even care right now.

Finally, Zane and I were escorted down a back hallway, down some stairs, and were tucked into the back of a police car. Not quite the limo I'd started my evening in. Life had a way of humbling you.

The paparazzi hadn't seen us, so that was good. I only hoped they weren't waiting at my house. Since I was renting, I figured it would be harder for people to track me down.

I could be wrong.

I often was. Usually more times than not.

Neither Zane nor I said very much as Officer Byron—also called Officer Always Serious—started down the road. It was dark outside. I glanced at the time on the dashboard: 1:30 a.m. It had been a long, long evening, and it was late enough that there was hardly anyone else on the road.

At least I was able to go home. Unlike Carli or Tim.

I glanced out the window, and my head swerved.

I blinked.

Certainly I was seeing things.

But I thought I'd spotted the person from the premiere who wore that mask with my face on it.

The woman—or man? I couldn't tell—was on the side of the road. Not walking. Just standing there. He or she appeared to be staring. At us.

At me.

A shiver ran up my spine.

It was most likely just my imagination and stress cohabitating together in my head.

That was probably it. I didn't even mention it because I would probably only sound crazier than I already did.

Silence still stretched. Zane played on his phone, and Officer Byron remained quiet.

What was there to say after the events of tonight? I was still processing and thinking and coming up with a mental list of suspects. It was a terrible list thus far. I definitely needed more to go on.

No reputable detective would put Rutherford and Eric at the top of the list. It was emotional and nonsensical. Sherlock Holmes wouldn't approve. Nor would Adrian Monk or Harriet the Spy.

Officer Byron pulled up to the house and opened my

door. He nodded his farewell, and Zane and I started toward the duplex where we were both staying—each in different sides. The walk from the car to the door wasn't long, but it felt like a mile.

I perused everything around us. The looming beach houses. The fortress-like dunes near the ocean. The cars parked at the street.

Was danger looming anywhere?

I didn't know, and I didn't want to stand around and find out. Thankfully, Zane stayed close and kept an arm around my waist. I could feel the tension coming from him also.

As soon as we stepped inside my house, I released my breath. Maybe I was safe in here.

"How about if I go fix us some dinner?" Zane said. "Are you hungry?"

"Now that you mention it, I am."

"You sit and relax. Let me fix something."

I didn't feel up to arguing, so I sat on the couch and turned on the TV.

It just happened to be on one of those twenty-four-hour news stations. A story was airing about how I was critically injured at the event today. Footage of the movie premiere's opening scrolled across the screen.

Sure enough, it looked just like me breaking through that fake movie screen. Just like the scene from my domestic spy flick, which was kind of like the *Bourne Identity*, only with girls and less violence and cute clothes.

"I know this is a big disappointment to you." Zane lowered himself beside me and handed me a smoothie. "Would Bob Ross help?"

I shook my head. "Not even Bob and his happy little accidents would help right now, unfortunately."

"A massage?"

I shook my head again. "Not even a massage. But I will try this smoothie."

"It's pineapple, mango, spinach, and cashews."

"Sounds delish."

"Glad I could be of service."

I took a sip, and my thoughts wound tighter inside me. "What if someone *did* mean for that to be me, Zane?"

He stretched his arm across the back of the couch. "I don't know, Joey. That's a pretty dramatic way of doing things, wouldn't you say?"

"There are definitely easier ways to hurt someone. Unless it was a member of the crew, someone would have had to sneak backstage to sabotage that harness. It would have been easy for them to get caught."

"It's true. It was a big risk."

I frowned as my thoughts continued their very confusing journey.

"But then I think about the people who were back there, and I hate to think they're guilty. Mostly they're people I know."

"I get that, Joey. I'm sorry."

At least there was Helena, the woman Tim had mentioned to me. I needed to somehow find her and talk to her.

As the thought settled in my mind, I realized one thing. I was going to get to the bottom of this if it was the last thing I did.

Not for my sake, but Carli's.

———

I'd hardly slept all night. How could I when my friend was

in the hospital? Instead, my mind raced through possibilities as to what had happened. But I came up short. I had no idea who would do this—who would be willing to take things this far. I'd like to believe it was no one I knew, but I couldn't say that with 100 percent confidence—not until I knew for sure who the intended target was. At this point it was a toss-up.

I walked downstairs at 6:00 a.m. and saw Zane snoozing on the couch, a fleece blanket drawn around his shoulders. As soon as my foot hit the bottom step, he sat up straight. When he saw me, he released his breath. He ran a hand through his curly hair and then shook it, sending tendrils flying all around his face.

He'd grown his hair out over the past few weeks, and to my horror, he'd worn a man bun on more than one occasion.

"Morning," I called, standing beside the couch in my running shorts, pink tank top, and sneakers.

He ran a hand over his face, obviously not a morning person. "What are you doing up so early?"

"Can't sleep. Want to go on a run?"

He paused for one more minute before throwing the blanket off and stretching. "Yeah, that would be good."

Zane and I had become work-out buddies lately. We were more than work-out buddies. We were marking things off his bucket list, which he was completing as part of a deal he had with a local surf shop. They sponsored him to document his adventures, as long as he featured products from their store in the process.

So far we'd climbed a lighthouse at sunset and searched for the infamous Goat Man. We still had a whole list of things to do, including swimming with dolphins, rescuing a sea turtle, going kiteboarding, and exploring a deserted island.

Zane and I had an easy, fun relationship. I thought he wanted more. Okay, I *knew* he did. But I wasn't in a place to date anyone. Even if I was, how would I ever decide between Zane and Jackson? They were both great in their own ways.

Life would never be boring with exciting Zane. But with Jackson, I'd always have a rock beside me to keep me steady.

Zane disappeared back to his place—which was right beside mine—so he could change.

As he did, I grabbed a water bottle and took a long sip to hydrate myself. It was May and already warming up here in the Outer Banks—although there were some cool days sprinkled between the warm ones. The weather here always kept me on my toes.

Zane reappeared less than five minutes later sporting the said man bun, as well as bright-orange shorts and a yellow tank top.

Not everyone could pull off the look, but Zane could. The surfer knew how to turn heads.

"Shoes or no shoes?" he asked.

"No shoes, for sure." Running on the sand was hard, but at least when I was barefoot I could feel the smooth grains beneath my toes. Besides, there were very few places I could jog without shoes. Certainly not down the sidewalk or the street.

There was no mistake about it—I didn't look like someone from *Baywatch* as I jogged down the shore. But that was okay. I was trying to remain fit and healthy, and exercise helped me avoid seeing a shrink.

I stepped outside, and the warmth hit me. If it was already hot at six, then I knew I was in for a scorcher today. I readjusted my ponytail, making it higher on my head, and I mentally prepped myself for the burn of working out.

Zane and I went down the front steps and to a wooden walkway that crossed over the massive sand dunes in front of our duplex. As we hit the other side, the sun winked at us from its position over the ocean, promising a new day.

"Let's do this!" Zane said, his energy taking over and his morning sleepies long gone.

"Race ya!"

Before I hit the soft, loose sand, I began jogging in place and then darted toward the beach. But as soon as my feet hit the pliable ground, pain sliced through me.

My ankle twisted to the side as I tried to avoid whatever caused the agony ripping through my muscles and skin.

I yelped and fell back.

As I did, I saw the blood gushing from a deep gash in my foot.

CHAPTER NINE

"JOEY?" Zane knelt beside me, gently touching my leg. His gaze slid from my foot to the bloody sand beneath me. "What happened?"

Pain screamed through me, and my head spun as if I might pass out. "I think I sprained my ankle. And something cut my foot."

"I'd say." Zane ripped off his tank top and wrapped it around my foot, squeezing it to halt the bleeding. "I'll get you help."

"What did I step on?" I asked through clenched teeth.

He leaned away from me to get a better look.

"It's a broken bottle that was buried beneath the sand," he said. "It almost looks like someone set it up there in hopes of . . ."

Zane didn't have to finish his statement. I knew what he was saying. It was like the broken bottle was planted there. Like someone knew my schedule. Knew I liked to run barefoot every morning. Knew I used the crossover.

Was I reading too much into this? I had a feeling I wasn't.

I didn't have time to think about it as pain ripped through my foot again. I bit down.

"Come on. You're going to need stitches." He stood and hoisted me into his arms.

It was like Prince Charming carrying the princess off in a happy-ever-after ending. Only the princess was hurt. And she wasn't happy. And I had a feeling I was nowhere near the end of this.

At least Zane looked good shirtless as Prince Charming.

A girl had to stay positive.

I wasn't going to argue. I couldn't imagine putting any weight on my foot.

Just as we crossed over on the sand dune, a car pulled into my driveway. Jackson stepped out, and his eagle-eye gaze found us.

Of course.

Because why be humiliated once when you could be humiliated twice? And sadly, things usually happened in threes in my life. Did that mean Eric would show up also?

Jackson rushed toward me. Actually, he wasn't a rusher. He was always cool and in control. Unflappable. But this time, his steady steps were urgent. "What happened?"

"Someone left a bottle—broken side up—buried in the sand dune right where the walkway ends," Zane explained. "Joey got cut pretty deep and twisted her ankle in the process. I'm going to take her to the ER."

"I said I'm fine." But my voice belied my words. I was in agony.

And I hated hospitals. I hated needles. I hated pain.

Really, I'd be okay with passing out and waking up when this was all over.

"Put her in my car," Jackson said, striding toward it and opening the back door. "I'll drive her there."

Zane didn't argue. Probably because his vehicle of choice was a camper van that didn't start half the time.

"I'll be right there," Jackson said, jogging toward the beach.

What was he doing?

As Zane settled me in the back, my foot still raised, Jackson returned with the broken bottle placed in a paper bag. At least, that was what I assumed was inside. And did he always carry evidence bags with him? Or was it just around me? Strangely, I wasn't unconvinced that it couldn't be a possibility.

"You think someone did this on purpose also, don't you?" I asked, wishing the pain would stop throbbing in my foot. And wishing my worst-case scenarios would remain scenarios and not reality.

He climbed in and slammed the door. "I think it's a possibility. I'm taking this, just in case there are any fingerprints. The way it was placed certainly makes it appear that this wasn't an accident. There were four bottles, which definitely seems purposeful."

My throat clenched. Four of them? Someone wanted to make sure they hit their intended target. Someone wanted to make sure I was caught in their trap.

I didn't like the sound of that. He was confirming what I already thought.

I glanced down at my foot and felt woozy when I saw the red stain spreading on Zane's yellow shirt. I closed my eyes, but the image wouldn't leave my mind.

"I'm bleeding all over your seat," I said. "And all over Zane's shirt."

"It will be fine," Jackson said. "Let's just worry about getting you stitched up."

I didn't have energy to argue. We took off down the

road. Jackson turned on his lights but kept his siren off. This wasn't an emergency. But the sooner I got this gash stitched up, the better.

"How's Carli?" I asked through clenched teeth.

"Still the same," Jackson said. "They're keeping her sedated."

"Any leads?" I continued, hoping if I thought about someone else that my own pain would be forgotten. As if.

"Not yet. Worry about that later. Right now, let's get you fixed."

Thankfully, the hospital wasn't far away and traffic wasn't heavy.

As Jackson pulled to a stop at the ER entrance, Zane scooped me into his arms and carried me inside. I supposed it was quicker than getting a wheelchair or watching me hobble.

But I had to admit I felt as if I was making a spectacle of myself. I was an actress. I was supposed to be the center of attention. But I really only liked being an attention hog when it was on purpose, not when someone else forced it on me.

Zane set me in a gray padded chair and went to sign me in—which really meant he brought back a ton of paperwork for me to fill out. Thankfully, I had saved my insurance information on my cell phone.

After Jackson parked, he joined us. He sat on the other side of me, bringing me a table so I could prop my aching foot up. At least the bleeding seemed to have stopped or slowed. I was afraid to check.

As I filled in my insurance information, I remembered something Zane had told me a couple of days ago.

"Don't you have someone coming into town to look at

houses?" I asked. "You were super excited about it because he's a high-interest customer."

Zane shrugged. "I can hand it off to another realtor. No big deal."

"Don't be ridiculous," I said. Paying bills was a big deal. A really big deal. "I'll be fine."

Zane was a part-time realtor, a part-time massage therapist, a part-time surfboard repairer, and an any-time-possible surfer.

People did what they could to make a living in this area. Most didn't seem to mind having a hodgepodge of jobs, not if it meant living in their dream location.

"I'll stay with her," Jackson said.

I expected Zane to argue, but to my surprise, he stood. "Are you sure?"

"I'm sure," I said.

"If you don't mind, maybe I will keep this appointment," he said. "And I guess I should go home to change so I can at least be wearing a shirt."

Now that he mentioned it, I had seen several women staring at us. And why not? Zane was bronzed, lean, and smooth. No one was complaining.

"You want this one back?" I nodded toward the bloody tank top, just to be polite and slightly ridiculous.

"That would make a statement. A serial-killer type of statement. I'll pass."

I squeezed out a smile. "Thanks for your help, Zane. Do you have a way of getting home?"

"It's not that far. I can walk. Otherwise, I'll call someone for a ride." His gaze shifted to Jackson, and doubt flashed in his eyes. As soon as the emotion appeared, it was gone. "I'll check in with you later. Take care of her."

Jackson didn't acknowledge Zane's order. He wasn't the

type who let people boss him around, unless they were people who were supposed to boss him around. Like the mayor or the police chief.

I closed my eyes as my foot throbbed even harder. I was such a sissy, and I knew it.

As another pulse of pain ripped through me, I let out a little cry and shut my eyes again. This was going to be a long wait, wasn't it?

Jackson dropped off my paperwork for me and then sat back down. He leaned close, his gaze watching everyone around us—like always. He was never really off duty. "So I've spent quite a bit of time here in the ER."

I turned toward him, surprised at his statement. "Have you?"

"As a cop, I have to bring people in on occasion."

"That makes sense."

"I've seen some strange things," Jackson said.

"Like what?" This would be a good distraction.

He rested an elbow on the armrest between us, looking surprisingly laid back. "Once this woman called 911 but didn't say anything. We are obligated to check out every call, so we went to her house. She answered wearing a gas mask."

"A gas mask?"

"Yeah, a full-on gas mask that covered her whole face, the kind you see in end-of-the-world apocalypse movies."

"What happened?"

"Well, it was hard to know because of the mask. We couldn't understand what she was saying, but she was acting crazy, so we decided to have her checked out. It turned out she had pneumonia. She was trying to prevent us from getting sick."

"Oh my."

"I had to bring another man one time. He'd called 911 and said he was having a heart attack. I got to his place, and he was butt naked. Refused to get dressed. Said he didn't believe in clothes."

I giggled. "What did you do?"

"We brought him to the ER and tried to keep a blanket around him. It was a challenge, to say the least."

"No way," I said.

"Way."

He told me a few more ER stories. The thing was, Jackson wasn't a chatty type of guy. So I knew exactly what he was doing. He was trying to distract me. It was awfully sweet, really.

Finally, I was called back to begin treatment for my cut.

Whoever did this to me was really, really on my bad list. For real.

CHAPTER TEN

_____

TWO HOURS LATER, my cut had been cleaned and I'd received five stitches. My sprained ankle had been bandaged, and Dizzy had dropped off some crutches for me. The ER doctor told me not to put any weight on the injury and that I should check in with my primary care physician today or tomorrow.

Not putting any weight on my foot would make it really hard to investigate what was going on. Had someone planned it that way? Because I couldn't let this slow me down. I had to figure out who was behind this tragic non-accident.

After I was released, Jackson and I stood in the hospital hallway, and I attempted to balance myself on my crutches. Balance wasn't one of my talents, and Jackson seemed to sense that, because he stood as if he might have to catch me.

Part of me wanted to cry in frustration and exhaustion, but I wouldn't let myself do that. I had too much on the line right now. I'd cry when this was all over.

"You should get home and rest," Jackson said.

I shook my head. "No way. I'll keep weight off my foot,

and I'll hobble along on these crutches, but I'm not resting. But I understand that you have other things to do, so I don't expect you to wait."

"I actually need to do a few things here at the hospital," he said. "But I really think you should rest."

"I'm not resting."

"I know better than to argue with you," Jackson said, raising his hands.

He was really good at choosing his fights wisely.

I leaned on my crutches, my wrists and armpits already sore. This was going to be a fun day . . . not.

"I'd like to go and see Carli," I said, trying to mask my discomfort.

He pressed his lips together and offered a vague shake of his head. "I don't think they're allowing any visitors."

"I'd like to know for sure before I leave." I shrugged. "Besides, I'm already here."

He said nothing for a minute before finally nodding. "Okay, let's go then."

We took the elevator to the ICU. As I passed a hospital-grade wheelchair, I considered asking to use one. But I couldn't do that. I'd shown my stubbornness earlier, and getting in a wheelchair now would just dilute all of it.

I walked into the waiting room and stopped cold.

Eric and Barbie—I mean Tiffany—were there. Eric had flowers in his hands, like he wanted to personally give them to Carli. Or like he wanted any potential members of the press to see his good deed.

Jackson must have felt me tense beside him, because he whispered, "Stay cool."

I bypassed Eric. I couldn't think of any reason he'd be here except to gloat that he was happy without me. To remind me that all the mean things he'd said about me were true. To somehow silently scream to me that I truly was worthless.

He wasn't here out of the goodness of his heart, I had no doubt about that. After all the mean things he'd said about me to the press, and the fact that he was writing a tell-all book detailing life with me . . . seeing him felt like a nightmare that was happening over and over.

A doctor stepped out of the *Authorized Personnel Only* doors in the hallway.

"I need to talk to him," Jackson said. "You'll be okay by yourself for a minute?"

I nodded. "Of course."

I knew too well that all it would take was one minute for everything to fall apart. I didn't mention that.

I ignored Eric and hobbled straight to Tim and sat beside him. Actually, I pretty much fell into the seat there. It hadn't been graceful in the least.

Raven Remington would have forgone crutches and gritted her teeth through the pain. She would have probably stitched her foot herself, for that matter. Using sewing thread and a needle made from a peacock feather.

"How are you?" I asked, propping my foot up on the crutches.

He shrugged, looking like he'd aged ten years overnight. "The same. I got to see Carli for a little while this morning."

"What are the doctors saying?"

He rubbed his eyes. "They have to keep her drugged for a while longer. They did say they might bring her out of sedation just long enough for the police to talk to her. Until she's finally awake, we won't know if she'll ever walk again."

I squeezed his hand, a clash of emotions rushing to the surface. "I'm so sorry."

"It's not your fault."

My cheeks burned. Deep inside, I wondered if it *was* my fault. That was how it felt at times.

———

At some point while I was talking to Tim, Eric and Tiffany must have slipped out. The TV was playing the news again and showing a prerecorded interview with Eric. He looked so compassionate and kind as he spoke with reporters about how horrible this all was. At least reporters had finally figured out that it was Carli who'd been injured at the premiere and not me.

My gaze continued to peruse the room, stopping at the aquarium on the wall across from me. There were at least three dead fish floating there. Ironic, since aquariums were meant to be calming. Yet this one seemed to remind everyone watching about the fragility of life.

My phone buzzed in my pocket again. It was blowing up with interview requests. I'd address reporters eventually —once I got my head on straight. That actually seemed like a daunting possibility.

I didn't usually feel like I owed the press anything, but in this case I wanted to give tribute to Carli. She was suffering because of a stunt from my movie. I took that seriously.

I needed to look for a new manager sometime. Unfortunately, it was more complicated than simply asking someone. I had to find my contract with Rutherford and make sure we didn't break any of the terms set there. I'd probably need to get my lawyer involved.

This wouldn't be fun.

The good news was that even before I hurt my ankle and foot, I'd taken off work for this week. I worked part time at a hair salon since the IRS garnished my wages. It was a long story, one that was partly Eric's fault and partly mine, I supposed. It was more fun to blame it all on him.

As I hobbled out the waiting-room door and started toward Jackson, someone called my name. I recognized the voice.

Unfortunately.

It was Eric.

I'd hoped he was as gone as black-and-white films.

As I paused, my back muscles tightened fast enough to snap. My vocal chords took the brunt of it as I blurted, "What do you want?"

"What happened?" He nodded toward my foot.

He wasn't asking out of concern. He was just nosy.

"Just a little accident."

Captain Gorgeous shifted and looked around. "Look, are things cool between us?"

Fire ignited in me.

"Cool between us?" I finally asked. "What does that even mean?"

"It just means that I know things have been . . . awkward."

"That's an understatement. And by *awkward* you mean you're capitalizing on our divorce and painting me as a villain."

"That's an overstatement."

I wanted to cross my arms, but I couldn't. Not with my crutches. Not if I wanted to remain upright at least.

"You wrote a book, Eric. You've gone on camera to talk about it. You trash me every chance you get."

"It's just for PR. It's part of the business.

"Exactly. I'm a person, not a PR opportunity." Now that I thought about it, it seemed like everyone was using me for what I could do for them. Zane always got more likes on his social media when I participated in his bucket list with him. The mayor appeased my nosiness by getting me to do free publicity for the area.

Was there anyone who just liked me for me? Or was I just a means to an end? It wasn't a question I wanted to ask myself.

Jackson appeared beside me and took my elbow. "Everything okay here?"

I nodded. "We were just wrapping up this conversation."

"Do you mind if we have another moment?" Eric asked, scowling at Jackson.

"It doesn't matter if he's okay with that or not, because I'm done talking to you." I wasn't going to entertain this conversation anymore. "Enjoy your stay here in Nags Head."

CHAPTER ELEVEN

"THE MAYOR IS at the police station," Jackson said once we were on the elevator. "I know he'd like to talk to you. That's why I stopped by this morning, but needless to say, we were delayed. Anyway, I told Mayor Allen you probably wouldn't be up for meeting today, after everything that's happened."

My stomach sank. I felt like I was in trouble. Or being called into the principal's office. I'd never been one who liked to rock the boat.

"I don't mind meeting with him," I said, leaning against the paneled wall behind me.

"Very well then. You know, I saw the craziest thing while I was waiting for you."

"What was that?"

"These two girls walked past. Teenagers, probably. But they were wearing blue eyeshadow, all the way up to their eyebrows, and these little one-piece short outfits."

"Rompers?"

"Is that what you call them?"

I let out a chuckle, feeling halfway flattered and halfway

flabbergasted. Of all the trends I could set, that had to be the one? "Dizzy will be thrilled about the eyeshadow."

"I'm pretty sure they weren't copying Dizzy."

"Don't worry—I'll give her the credit." The moment was lighthearted, but my thoughts quickly became heavy.

"You sure you're okay?" Jackson stole a sideways glance at me. "You look shaken."

"I won't lie. I guess I am shaken. First Carli was nearly killed. Then the bomb threat. Then I hurt my foot. That's not to mention Eric showing up. That was just the icing on the cake." Before I realized what I was doing, I rolled my eyes.

The elevator dinged, and we stepped off.

"Why's he even here?" Jackson walked slowly beside me as I inched my way down the hall.

"That's a great question." I'd thought about it a lot myself. "It doesn't make any sense. He says it's because his book is releasing. He obviously has no desire to support me. Unless he wants it to look like he's supporting me, therefore making me look like the idiot in the relationship."

"No one thinks that."

I cut him a glance out of the corner of my eye. "You might be surprised. Eric is very persuasive. He's all about image. If I look like the bad guy, then he'll look either like the sympathetic victim or the strong, masculine hero. Either will work for him. As long as he gets attention."

A couple minutes of silence fell between us, the only sound the click of my crutches followed by the swoosh of my jogging shorts and an occasional soft grunt of exertion.

"Your face takes on a whole different demeanor when you're around him, you know."

Did I even want to know what that demeanor was? Of course I did. "What's that?"

"It looks like the life drains from you."

My cheeks heated. I couldn't deny it. Jackson was spot on.

I thought I'd been recovering from our relationship. With a little more time, maybe I'd be ready to move on and put Eric in the past. But seeing Eric here in Nags Head had set me back.

"When he's around, I feel all these old parts of me—the parts I'm trying to escape from—bubble to the surface," I finally said, slowing my awkward steps. "Since I came here, I've been starting to feel like a new person. Like the old me instead of the Hollywood me, but I guess the Hollywood Joey Darling is hiding deep inside after all."

"I know it can't be easy, Joey."

"I want to be stronger than this."

"You are, but that doesn't mean you won't stumble at times. We all do."

At his words, my crutches caught on . . . well, nothing but air, and I started to lunge forward. Jackson caught my elbow and steadied me before I totally embarrassed myself.

"Thanks. And I have a hard time thinking that you ever stumble. Figuratively or literally."

"Even I do, Joey. I have plenty of regrets and missteps."

"Well, I can't see you being anything less than perfect." Had I just said that? Out loud? I had to change the subject, and quick. "Anyway, I'm sorry you had to see this circus."

"Don't apologize. You do realize this isn't your fault, right?"

I trudged forward in another heavy, achy step. A wheel-chair sounded really good right about now. "I feel like it is. If I hadn't come here . . . if I hadn't agreed to this movie premiere . . . if I hadn't ever married Eric in the first place."

Jackson stopped me and scooted against the wall in

front of me to let others pass. He wiped my cheek. Was there a tear there?

Now that I thought about it, my skin did feel wet.

"Don't let him do this to you," he said, his voice low and intimate. "He tried to control you in the past, and he's trying to control you now."

I nodded as the truth of his words hit me. My cheeks heated as my throat went dry. It was partly what Jackson said and partly how he said it—in an up-close-and-personal way. So up close and personal that I could see the specks of green in his eyes as he implored me to understand.

"You're right," I said. "This is exactly what he wants. He wants me to be miserable."

Jackson stared at me another minute, and I could tell he wanted to say more. Something internal seemed to stop him.

"I really wish you'd let me take you home," he finally said.

I shook my head, although I was tempted to hide in my house like a recluse. I needed to talk to the mayor. And I needed to check out this Helena lady. Cleaning up this mess should be my top priority.

"No, I'm going to be okay." Determination laced my voice. "Let's go."

———

Just as I expected, Mayor Allen looked beside himself when I spotted him at the station.

Just as I didn't expect, Rutherford was beside him. My former manager had apparently set up shop in the bland meeting room. He looked a little too at home with three empty latte cups surrounding him and a man purse on the table.

My gaze zeroed on Rutherford as soon as I walked in. If I weren't on crutches, I would have marched over to him and given him an up-close-and-personal piece of my mind. But that would be unprofessional. Self-control was my friend right now.

Since I couldn't give in to my whim, I settled for, "What are you doing here?"

Rutherford looked up from a stack of paperwork. "The mayor asked me to help clean up this mess."

My gaze jerked to Mayor Allen, who nodded in affirmation and wrung his hands together.

"This is over my pay grade," Mayor Allen said. "And he so graciously volunteered."

Jackson squeezed my elbow, as if he sensed I might blow up like a watermelon with too many rubber bands stretched around its middle. I wanted to stay on the mayor's good side—mostly because he could pull strings that could help me find my father.

I just didn't know what those strings were yet. I needed more time to figure it out, which meant I had to tread carefully right now.

"What are you all proposing?" I used my acting skills and pretended to be more pleasant than I felt.

Rutherford picked up a paper. Probably some sort of call to action with three easy steps to follow. That was Rutherford for you. He always had a plan.

"We were wondering if you'd be willing to go on camera?" he started. "To offer your sympathies."

"I'd be more than happy to do that." I'd been willing to do that before it was Rutherford's idea. But I maintained my facade for the sake of peace and professionalism.

"People aren't happy about the event being canceled,"

Rutherford continued, picking up another piece of paper. "We'd like to reschedule it. How do you feel about that?"

Inwardly, I reeled at the thought. "Not until I know how Carli is doing. It would be . . . insensitive."

"Even if Carli doesn't do well . . ." Rutherford glanced at me as if trying to gauge my reaction. "We could still continue on in a way to honor her and let her know this all wasn't in vain. It's for the sake of the children."

Oh, he had to bring the children into this. Of *course* I wanted to help them. To use my celebrity status for good. I was back to feeling like that guy from *127 Hours*. Hello, rock and hard place.

"I don't even want to think about that now. It seems disrespectful. There's a lot of that going around lately." My words were targeted at Rutherford, and I hoped he knew it. Yet I smiled, purposefully trying to confuse him and keep him on his toes.

"Jackson, are there any updates on this investigation from your end?" Chief Lawson asked. He was a quiet presence here at the station, more of a hands-off manager who ran things behind the scenes.

The man was in his fifties, with a pleasant face, short gray hair, and amazingly unwrinkled skin.

I needed to ask him about his skin-care regimen sometime.

Jackson stood at attention. "No, sir. Not yet. But I assure you that we're exploring several leads."

"What happened, by the way?" Rutherford nodded at my crutches.

I cringed as I remembered this morning's events. "Someone left broken bottles buried in the sand outside my place."

"Ouch." Rutherford winced. "I've always said they should be outlawed from all beaches."

"That should be your next PR campaign."

Rutherford stared at me as if unsure how to react before finally saying, "I'll schedule a press conference later. In the meantime, Joey, could I have a word with you?"

Everyone's eyes in the room were on me. I wanted to shout no! But I knew it would only prove to hurt me—by making me look bad instead of Rutherford. I wasn't going to give him that advantage.

"Of course." I offered another placating smile.

"Feel free to use my office." Jackson's gaze latched on to mine. Something unspoken lingered there, and I wasn't sure what. I'd bet it was: if you need me, I'll be close. Jackson was just that kind of guy.

CHAPTER TWELVE

I HOBBLED into Jackson's office and eyeballed his comfy leather desk chair. I really wanted to sit down, but Raven 101 had taught me enough about body language to know that sitting would make me seem weaker. Especially if Rutherford remained standing.

That wasn't going to happen.

Instead, I comforted myself with Jackson's familiar scent as well as his simple, clean office. The uncluttered space made my mind feel uncluttered as well.

I turned to Rutherford.

"What do you want, Rutherford?" My voice didn't contain the edge of anger I thought it might. Instead, it sounded flat and resigned.

"Look, Joey, I'm sorry about what happened." Rutherford hunched his back, and his shoulders drooped as he turned toward me. "Perhaps I didn't use good judgment."

"Not by any stretch of the imagination." And had he been taking some acting classes? Because whoever his coach was should be fired. The body language was over the top, and that annoyed me to no end.

"But we've been together for years. I've helped to get you where you are today."

"That could be debatable." I was uncertain if he really felt apologetic or if he simply wanted 10 percent of my earnings. He represented some of the top names in the business, but what he really loved was a nice paycheck. It made up for all the times he was bullied in high school. No, I wasn't making that up. He'd alluded to it several times.

He scowled, but it quickly morphed into a frown. "I just want another chance. Please don't cut me loose."

I readjusted my crutches, trying to maintain my balance and my self-respect at the same time. "You think I'll ever be able to trust you again?"

I'd trust him again as easily as Neo would trust Cypher in the *Matrix*. So. Not. Happening.

"I hope you will." He stepped closer and lowered his voice. "Look, I made a judgment of error."

My days of wanting to believe every apology was sincere were long gone. "You put a media blitz over my personal sanity, and now you want to call it a judgment in error?"

"How can I make this right?"

I raised my chin. "I'm not sure you can."

"I'm volunteering to fix this disastrous premiere pro bono."

"Well, that's kind of you, at least. But I hope you're doing that for the children's sake and not mine." I needed to hold him to his earlier statement.

He lowered his gaze, some of his softness disappearing faster than a conservative in Hollywood. "By the way, box office sales are going strong. It's the number one movie this weekend and has exceeded box office expectations. That's a very good thing."

"I'll take any good news I can get."

Rutherford released a long breath. "Look, I messed up, and I'm trying to fix it. I tried to get Eric to leave town, but he wouldn't."

"Why in the world won't he leave town?" Eric made absolutely no sense to me.

Rutherford began pacing now. "I have no idea. He said it's nice here. His career is tanking, and this is bringing attention to him. You know how some people are."

Yes, I did. I'd put Rutherford in that category also.

"Look, I let him go."

I blinked. "What?"

"I realize I can't work for both of you. I chose you."

"But I fired you," I reminded him.

His eyes implored me. "I hope you'll give me one more chance."

I hated the fact that Rutherford had gotten to me. But he had. Letting Eric go showed me he was serious.

But I wasn't ready to make a firm decision yet.

"I'm not making any promises," I finally said. "But I'll think about it."

"Thank you."

I looked at Jackson. I could see through the glass-topped door that he was talking to another detective in the hallway.

When he glanced my way, I motioned that he could come in. His hard gaze remained on Rutherford as he stepped inside.

"By the way, it's nice to meet you, Detective," Rutherford told him, his schmoozing side taking over. He was the best in the business because of that trait alone. "I've heard a lot about you."

Jackson only nodded aloofly. That look would intimidate the toughest of souls.

And I loved it.

Rutherford cracked his neck nervously. "Well, I'll be going. I'll be in touch about that press conference."

"Sounds good," I said.

I didn't breathe easily again until Rutherford was gone and the door was shut.

One thing was for sure: if I was going to do a press conference, I needed to head home and change first. I just realized that I was still wearing my running shorts and tank top and that my hair was in a sloppy ponytail.

What a way to make an impression.

———

I was incredibly relieved after I hobbled out of the police station and Jackson helped me into his police sedan. I needed some quiet. Some time out of the public eye—or the police eye. Everything had been happening at such a rapid pace.

As much as I wanted to slow down—my body was crying out for rest—I needed to find out who was behind all this. In a short matter of time, some of my suspects could be leaving town. That didn't give me many opportunities to question them.

Which brought me to a very important question. I turned to Jackson, certain that he realized the timeliness of this situation also. Yet, he'd been babysitting me.

"Why aren't you out there searching for the person responsible for this?" I asked.

Jackson cranked up the AC and didn't show any reaction. Nor did he take the car out of park. "Maybe I'm doing my part."

I crossed my arms. "No, you're not. Something's going

on. You're not the type to dillydally with stuff like this. You're the type who relentlessly pursues bad guys, like a bloodhound on the scent of its prey."

He said nothing.

Which made me realize something. "I'm your assignment, aren't I?"

He rubbed his chin and avoided eye contact. "What do you mean?"

I decided to cut to the chase faster than Tommy Lee Jones tracking down Harrison Ford in *The Fugitive*. "Have you been assigned to keep an eye on me?"

Again, he remained quiet. I took that as a yes.

"Jackson, you don't have to babysit me. I'm sure you have other important things to do."

Finally, he looked at me. "We have other detectives on this case, Joey."

"Okay, but don't you have traffic accidents to write up then? Speeding ticket to give out?"

"You really think that's all I do?"

"No! But I certainly think that keeping an eye on one person isn't really that important."

"You are important . . . to this area."

My heart sank. What had I expected him to say? I was being overly sensitive here. I'd blame it on my pain meds.

"And to me," he added quietly.

His words shouldn't have made me so happy.

"The truth is, this is Mayor Allen's request," Jackson continued. "You know how he feels about positive publicity for the area. If something happens to one of our most popular residents, it won't look good."

At least Jackson was giving me the truth. I could appreciate that, even if it wasn't flattering. "I see. So . . . you have to follow me around everywhere?"

"In a manner of speaking."

Maybe there was an upside to this. "Great, because I need to go somewhere."

He narrowed his eyes, as if he was trying to read me but couldn't quite get it right. "You should rest."

"I don't want to rest. I want to talk to someone. I *need* to talk to someone."

"Who would that be?"

I waited a moment, considering how much to say. But if he was going to chauffeur me around today, I couldn't keep this information to myself. I hoped Tim would forgive me. And that Helena wouldn't cause the carnie community to ostracize Carli.

"Helena Briggs," I finally said.

"Who on God's green earth is Helena Briggs?"

"She's . . . a lead," I said sheepishly. Had I forgotten to mention her to Jackson? Apparently.

He turned more fully toward me, no longer Mr. Laid Back. "How did you get a lead when I've been with you almost all day?"

I rubbed my neck, not wanting to insult him by saying that people weren't as intimidated by me—or they simply got me confused with Raven Remington and figured I was the genius I wasn't.

"Would you believe me if I said it was a long story?"

He tapped his foot. "I'm going to need a little more than that."

I remembered my conversation with Tim. "I promised not to make a big deal of this because it could be dangerous —or uncomfortable, at least—for Carli."

"Joey . . ."

I heard the irritation in Jackson's voice, and I couldn't blame him.

I was being vague, and vague was annoying.

"It's like this," I started, shifting my injured leg. "Tim told me that Carli ran into her psycho carnie friend, who claims that she just happened to be in town at the same time as Carli. They have a rocky history, so it seems too big to be a coincidence."

"Okay." He narrowed his eyes and waited for me to continue.

"But I can't let the psycho carnie lady know that Carli may have brought up her name because *Tim* thinks *Helena* will make *Carli's* life miserable if *Helena* finds out that *Carli* threw her under the bus. I guess the carnie world is like one big family, so false accusations could make things very awkward. Does that make sense?"

He ran his hand over his face. "It's pretty twisted. What are you suggesting?"

"I need a cover story."

"Okay."

He wasn't going to be any help, was he? Nope. He was letting me call the shots, which could be very scary.

"I'll just wing it," I finally said.

"That's pretty loosey-goosey, but you're the expert."

I scowled. "Do you have a better idea?"

"I'm just a lowly detective."

I slapped his arm. "You're enjoying this too much."

"Maybe I am. But I would love nothing more than to catch the person behind this."

I had to think this through so I wouldn't look like a total idiot. "We know how Carli felt about Helena, but do we know how Helena feels about Carli—other than competitive? If Helena is crazy, then maybe she thinks Carli is a threat. She has an alibi, but maybe she has connections. Maybe a crew member was in her back pocket."

I doubted my words as soon as I said them, but I needed something to go on.

"I need to remind you, Joey, that you could have been the target here. If so, Helena may not be the bad guy—unless you can think of some reason she'd have a personal vendetta against you."

"I know. But we should at least rule her out, right?"

He narrowed his eyes. "Probably."

"And you'll be with me . . ." It was more of a question than a statement.

"I will be. But I don't want you to think that means you're always safe no matter what you do."

"I know you have limitations," I said. "And I am trying to be smart and cautious, believe it or not."

"That's good."

"I'll call Tim and see if he knows where she lives." I looked down at my outfit. "This might just work after all. Until the press conference, at least."

CHAPTER THIRTEEN

TEN MINUTES LATER, Jackson and I pulled up to Helena's rental house in the neighboring town of Kill Devil Hills and parked across the street. This place wasn't one of the sherbet-colored mansions right on the ocean. No, this was one of the old-school home models that featured a one-story structure on stilts with a crow's nest up top to ensure renters would have an "ocean view"—and therefore pay more.

We stepped outside and onto the sandy shoulder of the road. The surf must have been rough today, because I could hear the waves crashing on the other side of the dune—which was on the other side of the street. With the sound came the scent of salt water, which I'd learned, since moving to this area, apparently healed everything. T-shirt slogans would never lie.

I wondered if salt water also healed sprained ankles and bruised egos?

As the sun beat down on my shoulders, I glanced at Helena's house again. I'd researched her on the way here. Helena Briggs was a part of the Briggs Family Entertainment Troupe. Interestingly enough, the family had a traveling midget act that they performed across the country.

As part of the act, they wore special costumes that made them appear to be height-challenged individuals. Their hands and arms were disguised to look like their feet and legs.

I'd seen some online clips, and I'd been surprisingly entertained.

They also had a background as clowns and could do some acrobatics.

Also interesting, they had a tour schedule posted that included a stop in Manteo—a neighboring town—for a children's festival that was taking place almost at the same time as the movie premiere.

Helena was looking less like a suspect by the moment, but I still wanted to talk to her.

"If it comes down to it, follow my lead," I started.

Jackson stared at me. "You do know that I'm the actual detective here, right?"

"But I'm your assignment."

He chuckled lightly before shaking his head all flabbergasted-like. "I'll humor you—unless I see the need to step in."

"I don't want Helena to think you're a detective, necessarily," I said. "We'll have to play that one by ear."

I stared up the staircase leading to her front door and sighed. "There are stairs everywhere in this area."

It was the ocean's fault. Everyone had to live above the flood level, or insurance companies wouldn't cover the cost of their homes.

"Yes, there are."

"I hate crutches and stairs."

Jackson turned around and positioned his hands near his waist. "Hop on my back."

"Really?" I questioned.

"Really."

I thought about it only a few seconds before giving in. Suddenly, I was in high school again and catching a ride with my crush. At once, I remembered coming to this area with my father on vacation as a teen. I remembered meeting a boy on the beach and having a weeklong fling. The guy—I couldn't even remember his name now—carried me this way along the shore at sunset.

I'd always had a guy in my life, but that wasn't necessarily a good thing.

However, at the memory of my family vacation, part of me instantly wanted to go back in time. I wanted to cherish those moments with my dad.

Would I ever see him again?

My gut clenched.

"This is going to be a workout for you," I warned Jackson. "I haven't been sticking to my raw-food diet like I'm supposed to."

"I'm okay with that. You probably weigh all of one hundred pounds."

"I did cheat and have french fries the other day. And I dipped them in ranch dressing. And I added extra salt."

"It's okay, Joey."

I'd been all in before my movie premiere. But sometimes I went from being all in to totally out.

It wasn't one of my finer qualities.

Jackson didn't even breathe that hard as he walked up the steps. I was fairly impressed, and I wasn't one to be easily impressed.

At the top, he gently lowered me near the door and

turned toward me as I found my balance on the crutches. "Easier?"

I swallowed hard, a lump suddenly in my throat. "Much."

Before I could stare into those intense green eyes of his, someone jerked the front door open.

"Can I help you—" The woman's eyes widened. "Oh. My. Flipping. Goodness. You're Raven Remington!"

"Actually, it's Joey Darling." I said that a lot.

The tall, painfully thin woman—she reminded me of Popeye's Olive Oyl—let out a little squeal. "Raven Remington is at my door! I can't believe it! Mom! Dad! Charlie! Andrew! Mary! You've got to see this!"

I exchanged a self-conscious look with Jackson. I hadn't exactly planned for this.

Before I knew what was happening, a whole crowd had gathered at the door, so many that I could see only partial faces on most of them. Paper and pens were flung my way. And everyone talked all at once.

It was a circus. Or should I say . . . a carnival.

I quickly tried to sign some autographs and answer some questions. Jackson kept a hand at my elbow to keep me balanced, which was good because every time my foot hit the ground, pain still shot through it.

I was trying to avoid taking too many pain pills. They might make me loopy, and I was already loopy enough without any medication.

"Can I help you?" Helena finally asked.

"I have a couple of questions for you." I glanced at the crowd behind her. "Do you have a minute? Alone?"

"Of course! Go away, everyone!"

A couple people moaned in protest, but eventually they all wandered away.

"Let's take this from the top!" one of them said from the other room.

The next thing I knew, I heard a chorus of munchkin-like voices singing "Shake It Off" by Taylor Swift. It was adorable, especially when I saw their dance moves.

Helena clasped her hands under her chin and beamed, totally and easily blocking out her family. "We're performing in Myrtle Beach next week, so we use whatever space we can for rehearsal."

"Sounds like an interesting life."

"Oh, it is. Anyway, I guess I should be asking what you're doing here. I heard on the news about Carli." Helena gasped, her smile slipping. "Oh my gosh. Is she . . ."

"She's okay," I rushed, realizing Helena thought we were delivering a death notification. "She . . . uh, she actually told me she'd run into you and that you were friends from way back."

Helena's eyes widened. "Carli mentioned me? To you?"

I nodded, deciding to go with that version of the story, especially since I didn't have anything better at the moment. "She did. What a coincidence that you were both in town at the same time, right?"

She slapped her leg. "Yes! That's what I thought too. Small world, right?"

I shifted, trying to figure out the best way to broach this subject. "Look, I know it's probably weird that I'm here right now—"

"Weird? It's great!"

"I'm just trying to piece together what Carli was up to in the hours before the accident," I said.

"Just like Raven Remington might?" She looked like a puppy dog being shown a bone.

"Yes . . . just like Raven Remington might. Did Carli seem okay to you?"

"Yeah, I think so. Why?" She gasped again. "Wait—what happened to her was an accident, right?"

I offered a stiff smile, remembering that the fact that foul play was suspected hadn't been revealed yet to the public. "We can only assume that. I just can't stop thinking about something Carli told me about. The accident that happened when you both worked for Darwin Entertainment."

I was totally fishing for answers, and I hoped it didn't come back to bite me.

Helena's eyes widened. "You mean when someone messed with the acrobat's line and one of them died?"

Um . . . I'd had no idea. But . . . "Yes, that one."

She shook her head. "It was terrible."

"There's no one here who would want to cut her line, right?"

"I saw her arguing with that guy."

"What guy?"

"I don't know. Right before we ran into each other, I saw her arguing with that guy with dreadlocks. Then she saw me and excused herself. Then her husband joined us."

Dreadlocks? That had to be Gerrard.

"That's good to know. Anyway . . ." I tried to think quickly. "We're going to have a vigil tonight in Carli's honor."

"A vigil—" Jackson started.

I elbowed him before he could finish. "I was hoping you might come. Maybe even speak."

Helena nodded, a little too eagerly. "Yeah, I would love to. Absolutely. Whatever I can do for one of my dearest friends."

I grinned. "Great. If you give me your number, I'll text you with the details then."

———

I could breathe easier once we were back in Jackson's car and I was off my foot. That had been a little rough. Not my finest sleuthing moment, but I'd had a lot of really bad ones.

"A vigil?" Jackson cast me a weary yet amused glance.

I shrugged. "It sounded good at the time."

"Don't you have to actually organize that now?"

I shrugged again, closing my eyes and letting my head fall back on the seat. I didn't want to own up to just how badly my foot hurt. "I suppose. Hopefully I can throw this together rather quickly. How hard can it be?"

"Yeah, I hope so. I'm not really as good at this winging-it thing as you are."

"We all have different talents."

"I guess so."

"Besides, what better place to look for suspects than at a vigil."

He nodded slowly. "You never know."

"Think about it—what better way to get a scoop about what's going on? The bad guy could come to gawk or gloat or do whatever bad guys do."

"You could be onto something." He turned toward me and crossed his very able arms. "What now, Detective? Is Helena still a suspect?"

He was enjoying this a little too much.

"Maybe. I need to verify her alibi, which should be easy to do since she was at a public event."

He crossed his arms. "So let's say her alibi checks out. What next?"

"Then I talk to Gerrard."

"Gerrard?"

The way he said it made me think he knew exactly who Gerrard was, but he was testing—or humoring—me. I decided to play.

"He's the guy with dreadlocks that Helena mentioned."

"And you know this how?"

"Because I get around—in a manner of speaking."

He nodded slowly. "I can tell you this: we haven't been able to catch up with Gerrard."

I flinched. "What?"

"It's true. He left the hospital last night, and now he's not answering his phone."

"That's suspicious."

"It is."

I shifted. "I'm assuming you guys have already questioned everyone who was backstage."

"We have. No good leads, but we would like to talk to Gerrard again."

"So you guys are struggling also." Why did I feel partly satisfied by that?

"Except for Gerrard."

Before Jackson could say anything else, his phone buzzed. That was a good reminder to me that I'd missed a call while I'd been talking to Helena. While he answered, I checked my voicemail.

It didn't surprise me when it was from Rutherford.

The press conference was scheduled in two hours.

I might need all that time to make myself presentable. I texted him back and let him know we should plan a vigil. He responded and told me it was a great idea.

At least we could agree on that.

It was a start.

When Jackson hung up and turned to me, I knew something was wrong.

"What is it?" I asked.

Was it Carli? Had she taken a turn for the worse? I prayed that wasn't the case.

"Forensics got back with me," he said. "The broken beer bottles that were outside your house were from Lightning Brewery."

That name sounded familiar. Even before Jackson added the next part, I knew where he was going with this.

"There were fingerprints on them," he said.

I held my breath, hoping I was wrong.

"The fingerprints matched Eric."

CHAPTER FOURTEEN

JACKSON WAS APPARENTLY LETTING another detective handle the questioning of Eric, which was probably a good thing considering all the twisted connections between the three of us.

I could appreciate that.

In the meantime, Jackson had taken me back to my house so I could make myself presentable for the press conference.

After he checked out all the rooms, he excused himself to make some phone calls. Through a bit of trial and error, I managed to hobble up the stairs on my crutches and into the shower. I changed into some jean shorts and a silky black tank top.

It was casual, but this area was casual. Besides, once I put on my strappy sandals that reminded me of an Egyptian princess—I put one on one foot, at least—and some jewelry, I figured I looked like a million bucks.

I took one more pain pill, wishing my foot didn't hurt so much. But it did, and that was that. I was going to have to live with it.

As I started hobbling back downstairs, Jackson saw me and quickly put his phone down.

"I should have helped." He met me when I was halfway down. "I'm sorry. I had a million phone calls, and I wasn't thinking."

"It's not a problem," I said.

He wrapped his arm around my waist and helped me with each step until I reached the bottom.

Then he still didn't let go, which I really didn't mind.

I hopped over to my purse, ready to put on the finishing touches for the evening. I found a little metal tin that I'd just received a few days ago and that I'd been meaning to try.

I rubbed my finger into the solid perfume—a fragrance made from wax and essential oils—and then dabbed it behind my ears. A soothing aroma surrounded me.

"I've been asked to endorse this new product line," I explained. "But I don't endorse things I don't like. This scent is called Island Breeze. It's vanilla and coconut. What do you think?"

He leaned closer. "I can't smell anything."

I stepped toward him, painfully—or was it wonderfully? —aware of his presence. Of every inch of him. We weren't touching, yet I could feel him. Sense him. "Now?"

He drew in a soft breath. "Nope."

I scooted even closer, my throat nearly closing at our near touch. "Now?"

He leaned toward me. So close that I could feel his body heat. So close that our skin—our faces—nearly touched. His leathery scent surrounded me until I couldn't even smell the perfume. Only Jackson.

My head swirled as I fought the temptation to get lost in the moment.

His face nuzzled my neck. Except it didn't. He wasn't actually touching me.

My breath caught as I imagined his lips brushing against the sensitive skin there. As I imagined wrapping my arms around him. As I wanted more than anything to be swept away in a pulse-pounding romantic moment.

Don't think like that, Joey. Stay strong. And never ask him to smell your perfume again. Bad, bad idea.

"I think I smell it now," he murmured, his warm breath hitting my skin and causing another round of heat to flush through me.

I sucked in another breath.

Did he have any idea what kind of effect he was having on me? Because my hormones were going crazy. It took every ounce of self-control to keep my hands at my side and not do something I would regret.

"What do you think?" I asked, trying to get a grip.

"I like it," he said. "It's very pleasant and subtle."

His breath hit my neck again, causing my nerves to go crazy. I closed my eyes, wanting more. But Jackson stepped back. A good two feet, at least. He cleared his throat. Stuck his hands in his pockets. Stood there unmoving.

My body sagged with disappointment.

Yet it was for the best. I had to remind myself of that.

Yet it didn't stop my breathing from feeling labored and my pulse from pounding furiously in my ears.

Maybe this would be a good time to talk about the kiss we'd shared?

Instead, I pointed behind me and said, "I think I should get some water."

He stared at me, doing the whole *smeyes* thing—smiling with his eyes. Thank you, Tyra Banks, for inventing that word.

"Not because I'm hot or anything." I fanned my face. No, that didn't sound right. "I mean, I'm just thirsty. Because it's warm in here."

His eyes continued to twinkle. "It is warm."

I backed up and nearly knocked something off the table behind me. I caught the seashell vase before it fell, and I managed to stay upright on my crutches. Yay for small victories.

"I'll get you too then. I mean, I'll get *you* some. I'll get you some water too then."

"How about if I get the water since you have crutches?" he said.

"That's a great idea." As long as we were away from each other.

When he was out of sight, I sagged against the wall.

This whole I-shouldn't-date-anyone-right-now-until-I-got-myself-together thing was increasingly hard. Part of me wanted to give up and fall back into my old habits. But I couldn't do that. I had to be strong.

For a little while longer, at least.

———

Jackson and I grabbed a quick bite to eat at Oh Buoy before heading to the festival area again.

He didn't leave my side after we arrived that evening for the press conference and vigil. I wondered if he secretly agreed with me that the potential almost-killer could be here.

It made total sense to me, and I'd be keeping my eyes wide open.

However, the scene was crazy all around me.

Reporters gathered, as well as other people who were just nosy or fans. It was a bigger turnout than I anticipated, with probably one hundred people. I spotted local news vans, plenty of cameras and microphones, and a row of chairs set up onstage.

No doubt the *Instigator* was here. Also no doubt they were plotting ways to make me look stupid. Maybe Eric had them in his pocket. If not, he really should become friends with the magazine's editor because they seemed to have the same life goal of humiliating me.

Just as at the movie premiere, the evening couldn't seem any more peaceful, especially with its location on the sound. The colors of the day's end were so peaceful and eye catching, a contradiction to the gut-wrenching reality of what had happened.

Rutherford prepped me. Mayor Allen wrung his hands. Carli's family had given the doctor permission to make a statement as well.

Finally, it was time to start.

I hobbled out to the podium, Jackson flanking one side of me and the mayor on the other.

Rutherford had prepared a statement for me, but I'd revised it, adding my own touches. I calmly read the words of concern and regret over what had happened. When I finished, hands went in the air.

"Ronald with *Hollywood Gossip and News*. Have you seen Carli for yourself?" one reporter asked. "Can you speak personally as to how she's doing?"

"I can't speak directly to that, but I can say that I heard she's stable right now," I said.

I called on someone else, and Dizzy emerged from the crowd, a wide grin on her face.

"I'm with *Hair R Us*," she said before clearing her

throat. "I have to ask—who did your makeup for the premiere? It was stunning."

I held back my smile. "Dizzy Jenkins from Beachcombers Salon here in town. She did a great job."

"What happened to your foot?" another reporter asked.

"An unfortunate run-in with a broken bottle on the beach," I said. "And the moral of that story is: pick up your trash, people. Or maybe we can work on banning glass bottles on our beautiful beaches here."

A few people cheered in response. I wondered if they'd had their feet cut on the beach also. Of course, my injury wasn't looking too accidental right now.

"Ms. Darling, Seagram Murphy here, freelance correspondent," a burly reporter with ruddy skin and ginger hair said. "Do you know how Ms. Moreno's accident happened?"

"I'm not prepared to answer that, but the police will be giving a statement when I'm done."

"Joey, are you dating anyone?" another man called.

My cheeks heated, and I shifted my weight on the crutches. "That's irrelevant to this press conference. And no, I'm not, just to end any speculation."

"What's next for you, Joey?" someone else asked. "Are you working with Jessica Alba again anytime soon? You two were dynamite on screen together."

My, oh my. These people had a lot of questions, and they were coming at a rapid-fire pace.

I might be an actress, but I'd never been good at this whole on-the-spot, speaking-off-the-cuff stuff. "I'm discussing my next projects right now. Nothing is firm."

"Is it true that you're going to bring back Raven Remington in a Netflix original?" the burly reporter asked again.

Had I seen him before? I didn't think so.

"Like I said, nothing is firm, but I'm talking about several projects."

"Would you consider dating someone?" the same man who'd asked about my love life earlier said. "I'm available."

The crowd laughed.

I wanted to laugh, but this shindig wasn't supposed to be about me. It was about Carli, and I didn't want to encourage this line of questioning. It seemed like we should show more reverence.

"Just one more question before I turn things over to the police," I said.

I called on another reporter, one I didn't recognize. The man was tall and awkwardly thin. His motions were also awkward and unusual—almost jerky. Definitely unpleasant.

And he didn't introduce himself.

"Joey, what do you think about your ex's tell-all book? Does it bother you that Eric Lauderdale claims"—the reporter looked at his notebook—"that you hit on his father and that Mr. Lauderdale repeatedly called you a sociopath?"

The blood drained from my face. Eric had said that I hit on his father? Had he put that in his book? I would have never done that to someone.

How could he . . .

Everyone was staring at me, waiting for my response. And I was giving them just what they wanted. I was speechless. My knuckles were white as I gripped my crutches. A vein throbbed at my temple.

And I totally froze.

CHAPTER FIFTEEN

I CLEARED MY THROAT, but before I could formulate any kind of response, Jackson stepped up to the microphone.

"That's all the time Ms. Darling will have for questions," he said. "Now the Nags Head Police Department would like to make a statement. But first things first."

Jackson helped me hobble over to a seat behind the podium, squeezed between the mayor and Rutherford. My mind still raced.

How could Eric do this to me? I knew things were rough between us. I knew he was a jerk. But I had no idea he would take it that far.

What else was in that book?

My stomach churned as I tried to imagine.

Jackson read a prepared statement that didn't tell me anything I didn't already know. I felt as if I was in a different world as I listened to the rest of the press conference. I needed to pull myself together and show Eric that he couldn't hurt me anymore.

The problem was, he could hurt me. I didn't want that to be the truth, but it was.

Reporters began hurtling questions Jackson's way. The first question I could clearly make out was, "How about you, detective? Are you single?"

Again, the crowd nervously laughed.

And for some reason, I held my breath as I waited for how Jackson would respond. My reaction didn't make sense, even to me. I mean, we weren't dating, so he could answer however he pleased. And I'd just answered the same question with a resounding no, so this was all nonsensical.

Despite that, I still held my breath.

"Let's stick to the topic at hand." Jackson didn't even flinch.

No, things like pleasing the masses never bothered him. I wished I had that trait, especially since there wasn't any pleasing of thus said masses. There was always someone who hated you.

"I heard that someone harmed Ms. Moreno on purpose," Burly Reporter said.

"Where did you get that information?" Jackson asked, a shadow coming down over his eyes.

I could see it even from the angle where I was sitting. Or could I simply sense it?

Burly Reporter shrugged. "A private source. Is it true?"

I strained to get a better look at the man. I wasn't sure if I'd ever seen him before, but he certainly seemed to know a lot. Too much?

"I have no comment," Jackson said.

"Was Joey really the target?" the reporter continued.

The blood drained from my face and left me feeling more lightheaded than I already did.

"I'm sorry, but I won't be taking any more questions on this subject." Jackson stepped back.

As he did, the questions began flying.

Jackson and I exchanged a look.

This certainly wasn't the turn I'd hoped this would take. And who had leaked information about Carli's harness being tampered with?

This had to be coming from someone on the inside. In fact, someone on the inside was most likely behind this . . . right? No one else could have gotten backstage without being noticed by security.

The uneasy feeling in my gut churned harder and harder.

Mayor Allen stepped forward and started with some generic jibberty-jab about what had happened, ending with some encouraging words and also announcing that they were trying to reschedule the premiere.

As he spoke, my gaze scanned the crowd again.

Had the person behind this shown up? Was he watching with a certain sense of satisfaction?

One person, moving through the crowd, wearing a base-ball cap and sunglasses caught my eye.

It was a woman. She kept her head low, like she didn't want to be spotted.

But something about her reminded me of . . . my mom.

At once, I didn't hear anything else going on around me. My gaze was solely focused on her until everything else was a blur.

Could it be?

I'd found a trunk my dad had left when he disappeared, and tucked into one of the pages of a book was a recent picture of my mom. I hadn't seen her since I was a toddler.

Yet I recognized her. She looked the same but older.

She'd left Dad and me so she could pursue a modeling career. We hadn't heard from her since, nor had she apparently become an overnight modeling sensation.

My heart panged in my ears as I watched the woman slithering in and out of reporters, headed toward the parking lot.

I wanted to go after her. But I couldn't chase her down. I could hardly walk.

Instead, my gaze remained fixed on her as she emerged into the parking lot.

She was leaving.

What if she was my mom?

And what if she had answers about my dad?

My adrenaline surged.

I started to stand.

As I did, something popped in the background.

Next thing I knew, Jackson threw himself over me. People screamed. The crowd scattered.

Was that gunfire?

Was someone shooting at me?

CHAPTER SIXTEEN

I COULD HARDLY BREATHE as I pressed myself into the stage beneath me. Jackson's body still covered me, ensuring he would take the brunt of whatever was coming our way.

But nothing happened.

My heart pounded as I waited. As dread pooled in my stomach.

But still nothing.

"Are you okay?" Jackson muttered in my ear.

I nodded, even though my foot throbbed with intensity, and even though I could hear the crowds scattering. Reporters hadn't been deterred—camera flashes were going off like a lightning storm.

"I'm fine," I said, already picturing tomorrow's headlines. "What's going on?"

Jackson pushed himself up. As he did, I caught a glimpse of fireworks going off in the background . . . during the early twilight hours.

Who did stuff like that?

Someone obviously.

"Sorry for our sense of panic." Mayor Allen rushed

toward the microphone again. "We have to practice the utmost caution right now. And I need to remind everyone that all fireworks are illegal in this area."

A few people in the crowd stopped and wandered back. As they did, Jackson helped me to my feet. I glanced at my hand and saw a large piece of glitter on my palm. What was that?

It didn't matter, I supposed. I wiped my hands together, then picked up my crutches.

Jackson led me backstage. Rutherford reminded everyone about the vigil tonight, which would start in thirty minutes. Apparently he'd already plastered the news all over social media.

Once I was behind the stage and out of sight, I released my breath and sagged against a chair. It was quiet back here. A police officer had been stationed at the edge of the area, just as a precaution. But I didn't need to worry about anyone cornering me or any bombs going off.

That was a relief.

"Are you sure you're okay?" Jackson peered at me until our gazes connected.

I nodded, still a little stunned. "Yes, I'm fine. I thought for sure those were gunshots as well."

"It would be nice if just one thing would go as planned," he said. "I'm sorry about what that reporter said about Eric's book."

"Me too. I never hit on his dad—"

Jackson shook his head, stopping me midsentence. "You don't have to explain, Joey. It's plain to see that your ex is desperate for attention and will destroy anyone necessary in order to get it."

I released my breath. Jackson understood. It felt so good to know that someone got it and hadn't been fooled by Eric.

He squeezed my arm. His concern was sweet, and I appreciated it. But I had other pressing things on my mind that I needed to talk about also.

"I thought I saw my mom, Jackson," I whispered.

He blanched. "Your mom?"

I nodded, my throat still tight as I thought about it. "I mean, I can't be sure. Of course. But I could just sense it was her."

"What was she doing?"

"Mingling? Blending? I'm not sure. As soon as I spotted her in the crowd, she turned to leave. Then the fireworks went off. I have no idea where she went. I lost her."

He looked off in the distance for a moment, his hands resting on his hips as a contemplative expression stretched over his face. "Why would your mom come here?"

"I have no idea. No earthly idea."

Before we could talk about it any longer, someone charged past the police officer toward us. The officer ran after him. "Sir, sir!"

That didn't deter the intruder.

It was Eric. And he stared at me with crazy eyes. "How could you sink this low?"

"Whoa, hold up, buddy." Jackson shoved him away, a hard look replacing his soft, compassionate one from earlier.

Eric jerked back and sneered at Jackson. Then his attention was back on me.

In an instant, I was back at my old home in LA. Eric and I were fighting again. And I remembered living through the lowest point of my life.

Distress seized me. My breathing became shallow. Sweat covered my forehead. My mouth felt painfully dry.

"Why would you do something like that?" Eric

demanded, his nostrils flaring as he stared over Jackson's shoulder at me.

"I have no idea what you're talking about," I said.

Jackson wedged himself farther between me and Eric, a fact I immensely appreciated.

"You told the police that I did this to you?" He stared at my foot like an alien might burst from the appendage and eat him alive. "That I planted bottles in the sand outside your house?"

"I didn't tell the police that," I said.

It was too bad the police hadn't had enough evidence to hold him. Jackson had told me earlier that Tiffany was Eric's alibi and had claimed she and Eric had been out all night partying. Police were verifying that right now.

"You need to back off," Jackson growled, and I could see the muscles rippling beneath his shirt. "I'm sure it was explained to you that your fingerprints were found on those bottles."

"She planted them there." Eric sneered at me again, trying to lean past Jackson to get in my face. "One more thing she initiated to try and ruin me."

"If I wanted to ruin you, I could," I shot back.

I'd kept quiet about everything he did to me. I didn't want people to know my personal business, but he was taking it too far right now. If I went public about what he'd done . . .

"Was that a threat?" He glared at me, his teeth showing.

"You're not going to come here and accuse me," I told him. "You've got some nerve after everything you've done."

Fire flared to life in his eyes, moving from campfire status to blazing inferno. "You're the one who made my life miserable. And now Rutherford dumped me as his client. I can't wait for my book to release this weekend. Then things are going to turn around for me."

That same fire wanted to ignite in me, but Eric was egging me on. He wanted me to get fired up. I couldn't give him that satisfaction.

"I'm not having this conversation anymore," I said instead.

"Because you know I'm right." His eyes were still bulging, his tone haughty, and he was making Hannibal Lecter look like a saint.

I wanted to lunge at him, but Jackson's presence helped me to remain calm.

"I guess we'll be seeing each other around since I can't leave town," he shot to Jackson.

Jackson glared back at him. "I guess we will."

Eric glared at me again before casting an afterthought of a glance toward Jackson. "I guess she's your problem now."

His words knocked the air out of my lungs. He was trying to put me in my place—a place of belittlement. Of inferiority. Of worthlessness.

It was what he'd done since the day our marriage turned sour.

Jackson bristled beside me, his muscles constricted.

"Eric," he called.

Just as Eric turned around, Jackson's fist smashed into his nose.

CHAPTER SEVENTEEN

BLOOD TRICKLED down Eric's beautiful face, streaming from his nose and into his beard and mustache.

He grabbed his face. Gaped. Let out a few choice words.

"I'm reporting you," Eric muttered, glaring at Jackson. "You're not going to get away with this."

Jackson hulked in front of me, a part of him I'd never seen before emerging. The amazing thing I realized was that he hadn't done it in a moment of anger. No, he'd thrown that punch on purpose and had known good and well what he was doing.

"Stay away from Joey," Jackson growled.

"Is that a threat?" Eric's tone sounded calculating.

"Take it however you want."

Eric straightened and nodded. I could see him scheming how he could use this to his advantage. A moment of fear rushed through me. This could be bad for Jackson. Really bad.

My messy life might ruin the life of someone else. Someone I cared about.

Jackson.

Eric wiped his bloody nose one more time before turning around and striding away. I watched him depart, and then I quickly glanced around. There was no one else in the area. No one had witnessed the altercation. The stage had concealed it. Even the other officer appeared to be busy talking to another officer just barely out of sight.

I released my breath as soon as Eric was gone, and I turned to Jackson.

Before I could say anything, Jackson muttered, "The man is a narcissistic jerk with no regard for anyone but himself."

"I know." I tenderly touched his fist, wondering if his knuckles would be bruised. "Are you okay?"

"I'm fine," he said, his eyes softening as our gazes met. "Are you okay? That's the question."

"Yeah, I'll be okay. But Jackson, you shouldn't have done that for me."

"I'm not going to let him talk about you like that."

I didn't know if I should melt or cry. "He can make your life miserable."

"I know. I've seen what he's done to yours. He shouldn't get away with that."

"I don't want to pull you into my mess." I squeezed the skin between my eyes, wishing I could rewind all of that. My Hollywood life was never supposed to come here, especially not this part of it.

Jackson gripped my arms. "I can handle myself, Joey. Don't worry about me. Okay?"

He waited until I responded with a nod.

But I wasn't sure that Jackson knew what Eric was capable of.

I was.

And for that reason I could sense a storm brewing in the distance. A storm I felt certain was headed this way. My stomach churned at the thought of it.

Someone slipped around the officers just then.

Burly Reporter man stood there. "Rutherford said I could have a moment with you," he said. "Ask the officers. My name is on the list."

Thanks, Rutherford.

"Any chance I could ask a few more questions, Ms. Darling?" Burly Reporter asked.

"This is a bad time," I muttered.

"You give me some information, and I'll give you some."

I stiffened. "Information on what?"

"On something very important to you."

CHAPTER EIGHTEEN

"THIS ISN'T A GAME," Jackson told him. "If you know something that's going to help out in a police investigation, you have an obligation to share, or I can have you arrested."

Burly Reporter shrugged, as if he could care less. "It's not about the investigation, and I have sources I have to protect."

"You're willing to give them up for the scoop from Joey, so don't feed me that garbage," Jackson said.

"It's complicated," Burly Reporter said.

Before we could talk more, a swarm of people surrounded us, including Rutherford and the mayor. They started a whirlwind conversation about the vigil.

The next thing I knew, Burly Reporter was gone. But when I looked on the chair beside me, I noticed he'd left his business card.

He was an entertainment reporter from *Persons* magazine. It was a respectable publication. Did that mean he was a respectable reporter?

What did he know? And who had told him? If not about this case, then what was it about?

I looked at everyone around me, wondering if one of them was the leak.

If anyone in my inner circle was that person, it was either Rutherford or Eric. That seemed like a given.

But what if it was someone I didn't even suspect?

The thirty minutes passed at lightning speed, and before I knew it, it was almost time for the vigil to start. Rutherford had prepped me. I was amazed at what he'd been able to pull together in such a short period of time.

Zane found me backstage ten minutes before we were supposed to begin. His name was on the list, of course. I almost didn't recognize him.

I'd seen him dressed up before—as recently as the movie premiere—but he looked even more respectable than usual right now in his light-blue button-up shirt and khakis. This must be professional Zane Oakley, the realtor.

"Hey, how are you?" He pecked my cheek with a quick kiss. "I tried to call you to see how you were, but it kept going to voicemail—which just happened to be full, by the way."

"I haven't even given my phone a second thought. But I'm doing okay." I didn't want to get into all of it with him right now. There wasn't enough time. I'd rather focus on Zane. "How did your showings go?"

His face lit. "A contract has been signed on one of the houses! I'm going to get a nice little commission off this one —enough to live on for a few months."

"That's great news, Zane!" I gave him a quick but wobbly hug.

"Yeah, I couldn't wait to tell you. We'll have to go out and celebrate sometime."

I remembered everything going on and frowned. "Yes, sometime. Maybe when I can walk again."

He frowned also as he glanced at my foot. "That's such a bummer."

"Tell me about it."

He scanned the area around us. I could hear the crowd in the distance, and I knew I needed to mentally prepare myself for this event. I was exhausted, and I'd love nothing more than to go home and relax. But that wasn't on my schedule right now.

"Looks like your manager is motioning to you," Zane said.

I glanced up and spotted Rutherford. "I'll talk to you later, okay?"

"Break a leg." He grimaced and glanced at my ankle. "Or so to speak."

———

The evening started with Rutherford reading a poem to a very attentive crowd of probably five hundred people. Most of them held candles or turned on the lights on their cell phones. A quiet calm surrounded the gathering, as if they wanted to pay proper respect.

Rutherford's poem quickly moved into a video presentation of Carli. Carli in all her blockbuster movies. Celebrities were on camera offering their condolences. Even Jessica Alba and Anne Hathaway.

A local band had agreed to play during an unsilent moment of silence. Their melody was haunting, and I couldn't stop replaying the scene from the premiere. The horror of finding Carli on the ground.

Instead, I concentrated on the crowd. Was the killer here? Was he or she staring up at the stage right now?

The fact remained that crowds were good . . . unless you were in danger. Then crowds were bad. Very bad.

Based on Jackson's body language, he agreed with me.

My thoughts went back to that punch he'd given Eric earlier.

In one way, it was comforting to have someone stand up for me. Jackson was always that guy. I knew he'd be in my corner. On the other hand, a million and one scenarios of everything that could go wrong fluttered through my mind.

What if Eric took this to the press? What if he put one of his spins on the story? What if he tried to ruin Jackson just like he ruined anyone who got in his way? I could hardly stomach the thought of it.

"Joey, you're on," someone called to me.

I felt like I was in a trance as I went out onstage, but I did what was expected of me. I spoke from my heart. I prayed. I had a moment of silence.

Then Tim spoke, telling about how they met and how much Carli meant to him.

I glanced out in the audience. Was the bad guy here? I thought there was a good chance he was. But who?

Gerrard? I really had so very few suspects.

One person did catch my eye.

It was the man or woman wearing that ugly Joey mask. Why would someone do that? And who was underneath the mask?

I hoped I had the chance to figure it out.

And then it was Helena's turn.

Helena . . . I'd nearly forgotten about her.

But as she took the stage, I saw the crazy in her eyes, and I braced myself for whatever might play out.

"Carli meant everything to me," she started with a sniffle. "She was always a beautiful soul."

Why was she speaking about Carli like she was dead?

My stomach clenched with unease.

"She could light up any room, and all the attention was suddenly on her. All the time . . ." A bitter edge entered her voice.

"Something's not right with her," Jackson whispered.

I nodded. "I know."

And this was all my idea. If anything went wrong, guess who would be to blame? Yep, that was right. Me again.

I was a magnet for these kinds of things.

"Let's do this tonight in memory of Carli Moreno," she ended.

Memory? Wasn't that reserved for people who were dead?

Okay, I had to get this back under control.

I stepped up to the microphone. "I think she meant, in honor of Carli."

Jackson began escorting her away.

"No, I meant memory!" she shouted.

Oh my.

This was worse than watching *Jaws* before jumping into the ocean for a swim.

————

Jackson tucked me back into his car once everything was over. Though he'd normally have to help with crowd control, the mayor wanted him to keep an eye on me.

No more bad publicity for the area, I supposed.

I was so tired that I wasn't even going to argue.

Once we were in his car with the AC blowing, I leaned my head back and released a deep sigh.

What a night.

"The ER doctor did tell you to stay off that foot. You don't want to do any more damage," Jackson reminded me. "And don't forget to schedule a follow-up appointment with a doctor tomorrow."

"Problem is that my doctor is in California."

"I'll give you the name of mine here."

I closed my eyes, exhaustion hitting me like a tidal wave. "It's a plan."

"You ready to get home and rest?"

Home. My temporary duplex where I'd stay until I figured out the next phase of my life. The problem was that I had to move out soon because the summer season was starting and that meant the rent would double. I couldn't afford that. I really needed to look for a new place to stay, but I'd been so busy with everything else lately.

"Yeah, let's go."

Darkness surrounded us, creeping into every crevice of the car. We got to go to the front of the line, even as swarms of vehicles were leaving the area. Jackson didn't try to talk as we traveled. It was better that way. I could use some quiet to sort through my thoughts.

I had a lot to think about, yet so little.

I mean, I wanted suspects to jump out at me—not literally, of course. I wanted madly obvious leads to follow. But that wasn't the case for the investigation.

Helena had been a possibility, but she had a really strong alibi.

Eric's prints were on those bottles, but he supposedly hadn't arrived at the premiere until after the area had been evacuated for the bomb threat.

I wanted to talk to Gerrard, but no one could get in touch with him. I'd ask Zane about it when I saw him next. But Gerrard's silence was suspicious within itself.

I knew Jackson and his crew had questioned everyone else who'd been backstage, and no one had stood out to them.

What would Raven Remington do right now?

I tried to mentally review all the episodes I'd done as Raven, searching for one where she'd faced a case like this. Finally, Episode 306 came to my mind. All her leads had dried up also.

So what had she done? She'd kept pushing, and eventually new information had come to light. That was what I needed to do also.

Tomorrow was a new day. I was going to try and look at everything I knew so far with fresh eyes. Maybe something would stand out.

A girl could hope.

Something rubbed my leg on the floor, and I readjusted the way I was sitting. Maybe the AC was blowing something against my skin.

Then I felt it again.

"What is on the floor?" I asked, bending over to get a better look. It wasn't a paper. Maybe a half-full water bottle? Jackson was usually neater than that.

"There's nothing on my floor that I know of."

"There's definitely something brushing up against my leg."

"Here." Jackson flipped on the overhead light.

When he did, I spotted the source of my annoyance.

A snake.

And the creature was coiled at my feet.

CHAPTER NINETEEN

"OH MY GOODNESS!" I shouted, jerking my feet onto the seat as my heart pounded out of control. "Oh my goodness, oh my goodness, oh my goodness."

No, pulling my feet toward me wasn't enough. Just like Joshua Jackson was never good enough for Katie Holmes in *Dawson's Creek*. It should have been Van Der Beek.

And now I was living out my very own *Snakes on a Plane*—only in a car. I'd prefer *Dawson's Creek*.

I needed to get farther away.

I unhooked my seat belt and scrambled across the seat toward Jackson. The car swerved at my sudden motion.

"Calm down," Jackson directed a little too calmly, considering this situation.

"Calm down? There's a snake in the car." I stared at the floor. The snake was gone. What if it was crawling up the door? Or sneaking up behind me? Or . . . The possibilities were endless. And they all ended with me having fang marks in my skin.

I'd rather star in a vampire flick.

Jackson pulled off to the side of the road. In three

seconds flat, his door was opened, and I awkwardly scrambled across his lap to get out of the car and away from the snake. I moved amazingly fast considering my foot hurt like it did.

Jackson followed me a minute later, but he moved at a much slower, calmer pace.

"I don't see anything." He peered through the window as cars zoomed by us on the highway.

"What? What do you mean you don't see it? It was just right there." That . . . that . . . creature had been at my feet. Its scaly skin had touched me. And it had come from nowhere—just like Robert Pattinson's rise to fame.

This was the stuff of snake nightmares.

Jackson put up a hand to keep me back as he continued to circle the car.

"I'll handle this," he said. "Just stay away from the street. Please. I've seen too many pedestrians get sideswiped in my day."

"Gladly."

I scooted—hopped on one foot, to be exact—away from the road and toward the ditch on the other side. A ditch where more snakes could potentially be hiding. I decided to hop to a more central location so I could equally place myself between the danger of oncoming cars and wayward snakes. I was smart like that.

"I'm calling animal control." I pulled out my phone as visions of the snake biting Jackson paraded around in my head.

"Not a bad idea." Jackson still circled the car with a flashlight.

"And I'm not getting back in that car. Maybe not ever."

"That might be an overreaction."

I didn't care. "How did a snake get in?"

"I have no idea at this point. I'll figure that out after I find the snake."

I watched him search, my gaze fixated on him like someone unable to pull their gaze away from an auto accident.

"What kind was it?" I asked, recalling the stripes.

It was at least five feet long. It had fangs as long as toothpicks. Evil eyes.

Or maybe I should be a fisherman, because that was a slight exaggeration. It might as well be true though.

"It looked like a water snake to me, but I only saw it a moment." Jackson opened the back door and used his flashlight to continue searching.

"It could have bitten me." I shuddered.

"But it didn't."

"But it could have."

He looked up at me, his voice subdued but understanding. "It could have, Joey."

Another thought hit me like a Mack truck hitting an unsuspecting pedestrian. "Jackson, what if someone put it there on purpose?"

His eyes met mine again, and I saw the truth there.

He'd already thought of the same thing.

———

Animal control had finally caught the slithering critter—a red-belly water snake, they'd told me. The rest of the car had checked and cleared. Despite that, I was unable to relax for the entire ride home. I kept imagining that critter slithering near me, and the willies washed over me.

"You really don't have to stay here," I told Jackson as I unlocked my door.

"Until we know what's going on, I don't think it's wise for you to be alone," Jackson said.

"I hate to inconvenience—"

"Joey, I'm fine."

"What about Ripley?" I asked. Ripley was Jackson's Australian shepherd.

"A new neighbor moved in next door, and she's helping me when I can't be home."

She? That was interesting . . . and for some reason unsettling. Which was ridiculous. "That's nice," I finally said.

I took one more glance behind me. Zane had obviously gotten back home. I could hear music coming from his house, and a strange car was parked in our driveway. Interesting. I wondered whom he was entertaining over there. Or maybe he was doing a late-night massage.

It strangely bothered me, maybe because Zane and I usually hung out with each other in the evenings. It was crazy to think that would last forever. We both had a life outside of our friendship. Yet despite that, my curiosity was piqued.

We stepped inside the house, and I flipped the switch. Light filled the room, and all appeared clear. I'd never take that for granted after some of the events that had happened in the past.

Jackson checked the house before joining me again. "All clear."

We paused there in the entryway, and my heart began pounding erratically. It did that a lot around Jackson. Especially when he stood close. Like he was now.

Maybe after tonight, Jackson understood why I needed to wait before jumping into another relationship. Eric was a lot of baggage. Most actresses I knew were already insecure

—a lot of them, at least. But add an abusive relationship on top of it, and it was so easy to let self-doubt consume you.

I needed to go into my next relationship knowing exactly who I was. Not as an actress, but as a person. I'd lost that somewhere along the way. I also knew I was still healing and still trying to learn from my past mistakes.

The lines felt so blurry sometimes.

I lowered myself on the couch and raised my foot. It felt so good to sit down.

I expected Jackson to sit across from me, but instead he lowered himself beside me. Close enough that our legs touched and sent my nerves scrambling in another scurry of electrical impulses.

Then his arm slipped around the back of the couch, and my mind went the way of the rest of my body—into the clouds.

Why did Jackson have this effect on me?

I still worried about what Eric might do after their altercation earlier.

And I still needed to talk about that kiss with Jackson. Now would be the perfect time.

I opened my mouth, but Jackson spoke first.

"So I talked to one of my guys a few minutes ago," he said. "Eric claims that someone took those bottles from the trash can at his house. He also claims that it explains the fingerprints that were found on them. He thinks someone set him up."

I frowned. "He thinks I set him up?"

"We both know you didn't," he said, his voice both firm and bristly.

Jackson did not like Eric, which made him an extremely good judge of character. Right up there with Yoda and Gandalf.

"Detective Peterson also checked on Eric's plane ticket," Jackson continued. "His flight did arrive in Norfolk about two hours before the movie premiere. It would have given him just enough time to arrive when he did."

"Good to know."

"He also confirmed that the Briggs family was performing in Manteo for two hours before the movie premiere started."

The more I learned, the more I wondered if this truly was directed at me. I mean, I couldn't deny the bomb had been left for me. The bottles had been left for me. The snake had been left in the car for me. Maybe I should be looking at people who had reasons to hate me.

I leaned back, still trying to think this through. "What about Rutherford? I hate to think he'd do something like this, but . . ."

"Rutherford was with the mayor for most of the time after the dress rehearsal and until the actual event. The mayor vouches for him. The two are acting like they're best friends now."

"Go figure." Silence fell between us. "Look, Jackson, do we need to talk about the Eric thing?"

"There's nothing to discuss." Despite his words, his jaw flexed.

I could tell that Eric had really upset him.

"Someone needed to punch him a long time ago."

I rested my hand on his chest. "Jackson—"

He leaned closer and lowered his voice. "Stop worrying, Joey. I'll be okay."

Reluctantly, I nodded and began to lower my hand. Before I could, Jackson's hand went over mine.

"I think it's sweet that you're worried about me," he said.

I didn't know what to say, because all I wanted to do was kiss him right now.

But I couldn't do that.

Instead, he pulled me into his arms and into a hug, I tucked my head under his chin.

Being held by Jackson felt good. So good. Better than a kiss.

After a few minutes, I forced myself to pull away. "I should go to bed."

"Okay."

"There are two extra bedrooms," I told him.

"I'd feel better down here where I can guard the doors better."

I nodded and tried to stand, but ended up toppling down on the couch again.

"Let me help," Jackson said.

Before I could object, he scooped me into his arms. Instinctively, my arms flew around his neck.

Without so much as a signal of exertion, he carried me up the steps and stopped outside my bedroom door. He gently lowered my feet to the floor. I carefully put all my weight on one leg.

"You're going to have to take it from here by yourself." His voice sounded hoarse, almost distracting me from his smoky gaze.

My cheeks warmed.

I knew exactly what he was saying and feeling. What desires hovered in the depths of his eyes.

We both needed to tread very carefully.

"Of course." I pushed a hair behind my ear and drew on every last ounce of my self-control.

He took a step back.

"Jackson?" I called.

He turned back to me, and we gravitated toward each other again, as if an unseen force drew us together. His hand pressed on the wall behind me, and he leaned closer. Close enough that I could feel his breath. That his scent consumed me. That all it would take was a couple of inches and—

"Yes?" he said.

My entire body trembled. "I . . . um . . . I need my pain medication. It's downstairs in my purse."

He stared at me another moment before nodding slowly. "I'll grab it for you."

I gazed up into his handsome face and remembered our kiss. Wouldn't I love to re-create it? But I couldn't.

You can't, Joey. You can't!

Jackson stepped back.

"I'll leave it outside your door," he said. "I'll bring your crutches up too."

Yes, it would be best that way. I'd go to my room and close the door. When I was sure Jackson wasn't there, I'd grab my medicine and my crutches.

And the crisis—the temptation—would be averted.

I thought I would feel much happier about it than I actually did.

CHAPTER TWENTY

SOMEONE KNOCKED on my door in the middle of the night.

I plucked an eye open. Found my phone on the nightstand. Somehow managed to hit a button there. The screen lit.

It was actually 6:00 a.m., but it might as well be the middle of the night. It certainly felt like it.

Then all the events of the past two days rushed back to me. An ache pulsed through my foot and brought everything into absolute clarity. My life was a disaster.

"Joey?"

That was right. Someone was at my door.

Jackson was here, I remembered.

He'd slept downstairs.

And I was sleeping now. Well, I *had* been sleeping.

"Joey?"

I sat up, startled with new thoughts. What if I had drool that had dried on the corner of my mouth?

"Yes?" I finally called.

"Joey, I have to go into work," he called through the door. "Something came up."

I tried to jump out of bed, but as soon as my ankle slid from the bed to the floor, I froze with a new round of pain. I wouldn't be moving quickly to do anything. Hopefully, no serial killers would chase me. They would win.

Then I realized what he'd said. "Did you say something came up?"

"Nothing you need to worry about. I'll fill you in later. Listen, Zane said he would come by. I don't want you to be alone."

Jackson had called Zane for help? That was . . . surprising. Whatever had "come up" must be pretty important.

"I'll be fine," I said, staring at my bandaged foot with a frown.

"I'm not so sure about that. Besides, I'm not sure you can even get downstairs unassisted."

Jackson had a point. I wanted to argue, but I couldn't.

"Call me if you need me," he continued. "I'll be checking in."

I lay back in bed with a sigh. It was useless to argue. And my foot did hurt really bad. I needed to take more pain medication.

"Okay," I finally said. "Thank you."

I picked up my prescription from the nightstand, popped a pill out, and swallowed it. Maybe this would help with the pain.

A moment later, I heard the door close downstairs. Then I heard the door open again.

Zane. He knew my passcode to get inside.

I was going to have to get out of bed, wasn't I? I didn't want to. I wanted to pull my covers over my head and pretend like none of this had happened. But there was a sadistic saboteur or an unsuccessful killer out there. I couldn't take it easy.

I glanced at my phone again and saw it was already blowing up with messages and missed calls, most of which were unimportant I'd put it on silent last night so I could sleep, and that was either a great idea or a horrible one.

Another knock sounded at my door.

"Joey?"

It was Zane. I'd recognize his raspy voice anywhere.

"Hi, Zane." I readjusted the pillow behind me.

"We have a problem," he said.

"What kind of problem?" I didn't even want to know. I had enough problems as it was.

"There's a news van parked outside your house, and reporters are coming to your door."

I pressed my head farther into the pillow. Really?

How had they found out where I lived? And I was nowhere near presentable enough to face the press. The tabloids would have a field day with the circles under my eyes, and—I wasn't totally sure about this—but I might have the start of a double chin.

It was probably those fries I'd eaten the other day, the ones with ranch dressing. Had I mentioned I'd also had a Big Mac with them? Yeah, well I did.

"Tell them to go away," I called.

"I can try it." He didn't sound convinced.

"Tell them I have cooties."

"I don't think that's going to work."

What would stop them? There had to be *something*. "Tell them I don't think the moon landing ever happened."

Zane paused for a beat. "Are you on pain medication, Joey?"

"Maybe." I was okay to take more, right? Because my

foot hurt. I'd thought the bottle said I was within my limits. Then again, everything seemed blurry, and it was still kind of dark in here.

"Joey, are you . . . uh . . . are you presentable?"

I remembered the fact that I potentially had dried drool on my cheek. Not to mention bed-head and a potential double chin that had popped up overnight like a blackhead on a teenager. "No, not really."

"Would you mind getting presentable so we can talk face to face? I'm struggling here."

I buried my face under the quilt on my bed. It had been my grandma's, and it always made me feel better. "Bob Ross wouldn't care if I was presentable. He'd call me a happy little accident."

"You should probably hold off on any more pain medicine."

"Really? I thought you loved Bob Ross." Why was Zane so confusing to me right now?

"I do. So . . . about talking face to face."

"Fine." I threw the covers off. "I just need to hop in the shower really quick."

Too bad it wouldn't get rid of a double chin.

As soon as I stepped onto the floor, more pain shot through me, and I toppled to the ground with a loud, obnoxious thud.

The door flew open, and Zane stood there. "Joey?"

It was a good thing I'd worn some sexy stretchy pants and a gangster pug T-shirt to bed. Otherwise this could be awkward.

He knelt beside me and helped me to my feet. "You're not looking too good." He glanced at my nightstand. "How many did you take?"

"Just one a few minutes ago. And one last night. I'm

all good."

He stared at the bottle. "I don't know."

"Really, I'm fine. I just need a shower."

"I can't really help you in the shower. Well, I could . . ."

I raised my hand. There were some things that I'd only get help with if I was totally desperate. Bathroom types of things were high on that list. "I'll be fine."

"I mean, I'll do whatever I can."

"Zane," I warned.

"I'm kidding. I jest. Really." He raised his hand like an Eagle Scout. He was about as far from a Boy Scout as anyone I knew. He didn't like rules or confines or being told what to do. He defined free spirit.

"Just help me to my feet," I told him, flinching again at the pain in my ankle. "Please."

He slipped an arm around my waist and lifted me to my feet—or to my foot, I should say.

"Oh, there's one other thing I just heard."

I grabbed a crutch I'd left against the wall and steadied myself. "What's that?"

"Carli is lucid and talking."

———

It only took me an hour to get ready, which I thought was pretty good, all things considered. There were now three vans outside and uncountable reporters. I'd looked out my window and seen them.

This was so crazy.

With no one to help me down the stairs, I'd done the only graceful thing: I'd slid on my butt, step after step, dragging my crutches along.

It hadn't been pretty, but it had happened.

The noise of the blender had concealed my grunts, and no one was the wiser. And Zane hadn't asked any questions when he'd handed me a smoothie. I propped my hip against my couch and took a sip.

"I need to get to the hospital," I told Zane.

His eyes widened. "Your ankle?"

"No, Carli."

"Of course. Let's go."

I was already going to be raising eyebrows. What if the press had seen Jackson leave? What if they saw me leave with Zane now? The *National Instigator* was already having a field day with my love life. Now they were going to have more photographic proof that I was one confused gal.

No, I didn't feel the same mad attraction to Zane that I felt to Jackson. But Zane was a good friend—and didn't most healthy relationships start off as friendships? And we always had fun together. Who wouldn't want to be with someone they had fun with? Yet Zane seemed to go wherever the wind took him. Did that mean his love life was all over the place also? I had a feeling it might.

"Would you like me to drive?" Zane asked.

"Your van?" I pictured that.

"We can take my car," I finally said. "It's just going to be tricky getting to it."

It was times like these I could use Carli to give me some pointers on doing my own stunts.

CHAPTER TWENTY-ONE

BURLY REPORTER WAS STAKED outside my house, as was Awkward Reporter. He was the one who'd broken the news to me about Eric's book, so I automatically didn't like him.

I wanted to demand that Burly Reporter tell me what he knew. But I couldn't do that. Not right now when there were so many other people listening.

I also wanted to know why Awkward Reporter kept staring at me like he had a chip on his shoulder.

But I couldn't ask that either.

It was best if I just kept walking and pretended I didn't see any of them.

Hollywood had come to the Outer Banks, and I wanted to send it back. What I liked about this area was that it wasn't L.A. No, it was OBX.

"Joey, what do you know about Ms. Moreno?" Burly Reporter asked.

"Joey, are you dating two men?" a guy—I thought he was from the *Instigator*—asked.

"Joey, did you really hit on Eric Lauderdale's father

while the two of you were married?" someone else unseen asked.

My cheeks flushed. Zane ushered me into my car and shut the door before the reporters could assault me with any more questions. I heard Zane muttering a few non-laid-back things to the press and telling them to back off.

"They're vultures," Zane said once we were both tucked safely into my car.

"Yes, they are."

He pulled away, and we started down the road. "So any updates on the case? That one chick was crazy last night. I'd be looking at her."

"Helena?" I frowned. "Yeah, she was crazy." Crazy enough to try and kill? That was the question. But I reminded myself that she had an alibi.

"And she kept talking about Carli like she was already dead. That was weird also."

"I know." I frowned. "She has a really strong alibi."

"Do the police have any other suspects?"

My gut clenched. "I guess they're looking at Eric."

Zane's eyes widened as he eased down the road. "No way."

"Way. Those beer bottles had his prints all over them."

"Do you really think he would do this?" He glanced at me, looking like he just got the scoop on his favorite TV show.

"Do I really think he would try to ruin me? Yes. Would he take it this far? I'm not sure. I don't want to believe it."

"I knew you had a rocky marriage, but I had no idea it was this bad. The things that reporter said were in Eric's book . . . I'm sorry, Joey. I know you're a cooler chick than that."

I bit down. I hadn't told Zane all the details about my

marriage. The two of us had a lighthearted and fun relationship. It seemed like such a buzzkill to talk about some of
those details of my past. Something stopped me from going
any further with that conversation.

"It was pretty turbulent," I said, and I left it at that.

"I know we haven't had a lot of time to talk since we
went to L.A., but it was a lot of fun, Joey," Zane said.

I smiled. "It was fun, Zane."

And it was. Zane was up for anything. He'd gone to the
pre-premiere parties. The after parties. He'd smiled with
me on the red carpet. He'd looked handsome in his tux and
hadn't been overwhelmed by the attention. In fact, he *loved*
the attention. He could definitely hang with me in my
Hollywood lifestyle.

Could Jackson?

The question startled me. I didn't know. Jackson liked
quiet and peace and stability.

And I didn't know where I stood with that either. Part
of me wanted to embrace fame and go for it—to not waste
any opportunities. The other part of me wanted to get back
to a normal life, absent the paparazzi and crazy fans and a
demanding schedule.

The truth was that I didn't know what the future held
for me. I'd only planned this place to be a stop along the
way. I wanted to figure out what happened to my dad, and
then I figured I'd move on with the next step in my life.

I'd never counted on meeting Zane and Jackson. I'd
never expected to befriend Phoebe at Oh Buoy or to feel
like Dizzy and her friends should be a permanent part of
my life.

Most of all, I hadn't expected to ever consider the possibility that my mother might be in this area. Or that she
might have something to do with my dad's disappearance.

I had a lot to figure out, starting with who'd tried to ruin this movie premiere and nearly killed Carli in the process.

———

We got to the hospital, and Rutherford met me before I even stepped out of the elevator. It was my lucky day. Or not.

"You're going to have to wait your turn to see her," Rutherford said. "The police are with her now, and her husband wants more time with her. Plus, her family is flying in from Vegas."

"Good to know." I stepped into the hallway, dreading the long walk to the waiting room. It might as well be *The Green Mile*. Okay, that was an exaggeration, but it truly was exhausting hobbling along on these crutches. They made everything so much harder and more cumbersome.

Rutherford leaned closer, studying my face. "You're not looking good, Joey."

"Well, I'm on pain medication, and my foot hurts, and someone might be trying to kill me," I blurted. "How should I look?"

He backed off, raising a hand in the process. "I was just saying."

"I hate when people say that." I pulled myself together, realizing that snapping Rutherford's head off would accomplish nothing. "How much longer are you here?"

He shrugged. "I don't know yet. I'm still trying to salvage this event."

"How's that going?"

"The press is starting to get wind of the fact that Carli's accident may not have been an accident," he said. "While it's causing some great buzz about the movie, it's not so great if we don't figure out who's behind this."

"Who do you think is responsible?" Maybe Rutherford would have some surprising insight.

"A ghost."

I stared at him. "What?"

"Well, it obviously wasn't a crew member. That means someone else managed to sneak backstage. But who could do that? We had a fence up. We had security. We had people who got to the lawn two hours early and would have seen someone who was up to no good."

He had a point.

"Hopefully, this rinky-dink police department will step up their game," he continued.

His words caused my stomach to clench. I thought they were doing a fine job.

Before I could say anything, his phone rang and drew him away from this conversation.

"I thought people in Hollywood were charming," Zane muttered.

"Ted Bundy was charming."

"Point taken," Zane said.

"Hi, Zane." A blond nurse walked past and gave Zane a cute little wave, accompanied by an adorable crinkled nose.

"Hey, Zora." He glanced at me. "Do you mind? I need to talk to her about a surfboard."

"Go right ahead."

He slipped away to chat with her a moment.

As he did, I started toward the waiting area. Before I got there, Eric stepped out of the bathroom, bringing the fragrance of floral-scented soap with him. His nose still looked swollen, and I didn't even feel bad about it.

I was just running into all my favorite people while I was here today, wasn't I?

I couldn't catch a break. In fact, it all felt a bit like *Groundhog Day*—like the process of me running into people kept repeating itself over and over.

"I hope you're enjoying time with your little boyfriend," Eric growled, glancing behind me.

He probably wouldn't be acting this tough if Jackson were here.

"He's not my boyfriend." I wasn't sure whom he was talking about—either Zane or Jackson. But it was safe enough to say that I wasn't dating either of them.

He glowered at me. "Well, he's going to be out of a job soon."

I sucked in a breath at his words, hoping they didn't mean what I knew they did. "What do you mean?"

He held up his phone and showed me a picture of himself with a bloody nose. There had obviously been effects added to that picture because Eric hadn't looked that bad when he left last night.

He was even more vile than I'd given him credit for.

"You altered that photo," I muttered.

A calculated grin stretched across his face. "I've already contacted my lawyer. This is abuse of power. With all the negative press police have received lately, no department wants a head detective who socks people while he's on duty."

I fisted my hands. "You deserved it."

He continued to smirk. "It doesn't matter. That will boil down to my word against his."

"I was there too."

"Everyone knows you're not very reliable, nor are you objective. So it will be me against him, and I'm famous."

"Almost." It was a low blow but . . . maybe there was a mean girl buried deep down inside of me.

His smile faded. "You're a little full of yourself."

"No, I'm not. That was the truth." My voice didn't hold any amusement or teasing—I was dead serious, and I didn't want him to doubt it.

He stepped closer, his nostrils flaring. "You're just a little wannabe. And if you think that just because you had one good movie you're something special, you're wrong. I'll prove it."

I raised my chin. "You've been doing your best to do that, haven't you? You and I both know that one interview with me and the right reporter would sink your career permanently. No one wants to be associated with someone who hit his wife."

A glimmer of fear washed across his gaze, quickly replaced with anger. "You wouldn't. It would show you for the weakling you are."

I balled my hands into fists yet again, trying to appear calm, even though my heart stammered out of control. "I might."

"Listen . . ." He raised his hand like he wanted to jab his finger into me. But he lowered it as someone walked out of the waiting area. He quickly plastered on a smile, but it disappeared with the stranger. "There's only one way I won't report your boyfriend."

Instantly, my haunches went up. "What's that?"

He leaned so close that I could feel his breath—rank, if you asked me—hit my face. "If you promise to never, *ever* talk to a reporter about what happened between us."

I stared at him. "You're serious?"

"Dead serious. I'm trying to revive my career. I don't

need anyone listening to your fictitious tales and believing they're true."

"They're not fiction, and you and I both know it."

He glared back. "I have no idea what you're talking about."

Bile rose in my stomach. This man repulsed me in so many ways. "You are truly a more vile person than I ever gave you credit for."

He said nothing until, "So is it a deal?"

I thought of Jackson. I pictured him losing his job over this. His face being on the front page of newspapers. The fiasco would get even more attention because Eric and I were involved.

It would turn Jackson's life upside down. Even if Jackson insisted I shouldn't worry about it, I was worrying about it. I knew the lengths Eric would go to get what he wanted.

"It's a deal," I finally said.

A grin lit Eric's face. "I hoped you might see it my way."

Why did I feel like I'd just made a deal with the devil?

Probably because I had.

CHAPTER TWENTY-TWO

I'D GONE into the waiting room, fuming from my conversation with Eric. Zane still hadn't reappeared. But Tim had come out of the patient area, his eyes filled with a strange mixture of grief and relief.

"As soon as the detective is done, you're welcome to go talk to Carli—as long as the doctor says it's okay," he said. "I know they don't want to exhaust her, but she did mention wanting to see you."

"Thank you," I said. "Any updates I should know about?"

"It's still too early to know much. But the doctors are hopeful. That's all we can do, right? Keep our thoughts positive."

My dad would have said we needed to keep the faith. Faith had been the center of my upbringing, and those values were beginning to make more sense all the time.

A flutter rushed through me as I stared at the door leading to the ICU. I was nervous at the thought of seeing Carli. More nervous than I thought I'd be. More nervous than when I'd auditioned for *Family Secrets*.

Just then, Jackson emerged from the door. His eyes warmed when he saw me, and he gently nudged me away from any listening ears and toward the corner. "Everything okay?"

I nodded, remembering how loopy I'd felt this morning after taking my pain med. Remembering the fact that reporters had found my house. Unable to forget the fact that the headlines would soon be filled with Eric's lies about our marriage.

My thoughts ended with a recap on my earlier conversation with Eric and the deal I'd made with the devil. My life choices could potentially ruin Jackson's life.

I wasn't okay with that.

"I'm fine," I said. "Can I go see Carli?"

He nodded. "She asked to see you, but I want to warn you—she looks pretty beat-up."

"Okay."

He leaned closer. "Listen, sorry I had to leave this morning. There was a chance doctors would have to sedate her again if she was in too much pain. Detective Gardner questioned her, and I wanted to be there also."

"I understand."

He studied me another moment, his eyes probing, before nodding. "Okay. You're free to go see her."

I hobbled past the ICU nurses, nudged the door curtains aside, and stepped into the room. I sucked in a deep breath at the sight of her.

Jackson was right. It was hard to see Carli this way.

A brace swallowed her neck. Her arm and one leg were in casts. Her eyes were bruised and swollen. Uncountable machines were hooked up to her.

She looked awful and weak and nothing like the Carli I knew.

I put on a strong face as I approached her bed.

I blanched though when I saw her face. Looking at her reminded me of looking in the mirror at myself after my car accident.

The one that had happened when I'd tried to drive myself to the hospital after Eric left me for dead and took my phone with him so I couldn't call for help.

Those memories were just about as sweet as watching *The Notebook*—right after a breakup.

"Joey," she muttered, only her eyes and lips moving— and barely. "Thanks for coming."

"Wouldn't have missed it for the world." I touched her hand softly. "How are you?"

"Been better."

That hadn't been one of my most astute questions. "I'm so sorry, Carli."

"It's the nature of the job. Every stunt person knows that this is an unfortunate possibility." Her voice sounded weak and hard to understand.

Had anyone told her that this accident had been purposeful? How much did she remember?

Guilt pounded at me.

"I know, Joey." Her fingers tightened around mine.

I stared at her, unsure if I'd heard correctly.

"You know what?" That *Family Secrets* was a runaway success? That Eric was a jerk? That this whole movie premiere had officially been declared a disaster?

"I know someone might have done this to me on purpose. Maybe they even thought I was you. It's not your fault, you know."

"It feels like my fault."

"Stop blaming yourself, and let's get to the bottom of this. Unfortunately, I'm not going to be much help, so I'm going to have to rely on you to do the legwork." Her eyes went to my crutches. "I can see we'll make quite a pair."

"Yes, we will." I offered a faint smile, but it quickly faded. "Do you remember anyone being backstage before the premiere, Carli?"

"It's been all I've thought about since I learned what happened." She frowned. "So we did the rehearsal, and everything was fine. I inspected the harness myself."

I figured that much. "There was only about two hours in between the rehearsal and the accident. That had to be when someone messed with the equipment."

She licked her lips. "Rutherford was back there, but he was mostly with the mayor. Besides, he wouldn't know how to slice into that rope without being caught. Someone had to climb that scaffolding, and we both know Rutherford's not very handy unless it's with a tablet in his hands."

"I'm inclined to agree." Besides, he didn't have a strong motive for wanting either me or Carli dead. That would only serve to limit his income.

"There was a security guard back there," she said. "He seemed a bit cagey."

I vaguely remembered the man. I supposed being cagey didn't mean he was guilty though.

"Then there was a reporter who kept trying to get backstage for an interview," Carli continued.

That was the first I'd heard of that. "Was he big and burly?"

"No, he was rather awkward."

Awkward Reporter! Good to know. "What did he say? Do you remember, by chance?"

She let out a breath. "He wanted an interview with me, but I told him I didn't have time. And when I turned around, he looked confused. Like he'd thought I was you."

Interesting. "Did he leave after you talked to him?"

"I thought he did, but I'm not sure. It was all pretty crazy. Tim brought me dinner, and I wasn't paying that much attention." She frowned. "I don't suppose we've narrowed this down any."

"No, this has been helpful," I told her.

Her eyes closed slightly, and I could tell she was fading. I didn't want to press too hard.

"There is one other person," she said. "Helena."

I remembered the almost memorial Helena had done yesterday, and my stomach sank. "She spoke at a vigil for you last night."

"Tim told me." She made a face.

"It was . . . strange," I said, trying to put it nicely.

"She's strange. Helena has always liked movies. She tried to talk me into letting her come out to the movie set more than once. She wanted me to use my connections so she could get an inside look at some new romantic comedy I was filming. When I told her no, she got really mad at me. She said she was writing a screenplay and I'd just ruined her chances of going anywhere."

"I need to look into how airtight her alibi is." But I had a feeling it was super airtight.

"I agree."

I shifted, knowing my time was quickly running out. "Before the premiere, you said you had a bad day. Do you mind if I ask why?"

She was silent a minute. "That's right. It was that reporter. He gave me something. Because he thought I was you."

My pulse spiked. "What did he give you?"

She remained silent, as if mentally recalling their

encounter. "He got an advanced copy of Eric's book, and he wanted to know what I thought of it."

My stomach clenched. "Is that right?"

"The good news is that I took the copy from him."

My heart sped. "Where is it?"

"I gave it to Tim. He doesn't know anything about it. Ask him for it. I want you to see it before it's released."

I nodded. "I'll do that."

"You can do it, Raven."

I almost corrected her, when I saw her smile.

"You got me," I admitted.

Carli knew good and well that people daily mistook me for my fictional alter ego.

Her fingers squeezed mine more tightly. "Find out who did this, Joey. Please."

CHAPTER TWENTY-THREE

AS SOON AS I stepped out of the waiting room, I ran into none other than Helena Briggs.

I seriously had to stop running into people.

Her face lit when she saw me. "Joey! I had no idea I'd run into you here."

"I had no idea you could get past security." Oops. Had I just said that?

"Oh, I told them I was Carli's BFF."

I nodded. "I see."

"Now that you told me how much I mean to her, I knew I had to come check on her. How is she? I'm hoping I might be able to see her. I heard she's awake."

I fidgeted. "How'd you hear that?"

"I called the hospital, of course. And told them I was you."

"That you were me?" Had I just heard that correctly?

"Yeah, I figured you were on the approved list. I also figured it was okay since Carli and I are practically BFFs."

"You are?" I highly doubted that.

She shrugged. "I mean, it's practically the truth. We were like sisters when we were teens."

"She's doing okay," I finally said.

"I'm *so* glad." She drew out the word *so* until she sounded sickly sweet sincere. She leaned closer. "Look, I was hoping we could get together sometime."

"Get together?" I scrambled for an excuse. "Why would you want to do that?"

"I'm writing a screenplay."

"Are you? About what?"

"It's like *Romeo and Juliet*. More of a tragedy than a love story really. I find those to be more realistic. I'd love your input."

"Love often does end with tragedy."

"I meant about the screenplay, not about love." She shook her head, like I was an idiot.

"I know I have to stay off my feet right now," I said. "I need to go home and rest. Are you here all week?"

She nodded.

"Great. I'll call you then."

"Do you have my number still? I'll give it to you again, just in case." She eagerly scribbled it on a piece of paper from her purse. "Here you go. Do you think they'll let me see her?"

I glanced back at the waiting room, knowing good and well the answer would be no. "You could ask," I finally said, not having the heart to tell her what I really thought.

"Great. I'm going to go and see what they say. I hope we can get together, Joey. I want to write your next movie!"

Only if it involved dancing munchkins.

———

Zane was in charge of me today, which surprised me, considering that Jackson had said I was his focus.

But I supposed since I was under doctor's orders to stay home, Jackson had suspected I'd be okay, as long as Zane was there. I didn't have the heart to tell him that nothing was going to slow me down—not even a sliced foot and a sprained ankle.

"What are you thinking?" Zane asked.

"I'm thinking that my leads are drying up faster than a bleached blonde's split ends," I said.

"Well, what do you have so far? Maybe I can help."

"Right now, my leads appear to be the Awkward Reporter, an unnamed security guard, and your friend Gerrard."

"Well, I can't help you with the security guard or Awkward Reporter Guy, but I just so happen to have been invited to a gathering. Gerrard's best friend will be there."

"Are you for real?" I asked.

He nodded. "I'm so for real. Was Elvis the king of rock and roll? Not only that, but you might be able to get some R and R in the process."

That sounded perfect.

And maybe Jackson would even be happy about it.

As we reached my car, I saw someone standing there and waiting for me.

It was just what people did lately.

I sighed.

Even worse, it was Awkward Reporter, who had the inside scoop on Eric's new book. He must have followed me here.

"Ms. Darling," he said, straightening.

"Mr. Awkward Reporter."

He stared at me, looking confused. It only lasted a

second, and then he pressed on. "Can I get a quote from you about what's going on?"

"I don't really have anything new to say," I told him, eyeballing the passenger-side door, one that I desperately wanted to open so I could sit down.

"Is someone trying to sabotage your movie premiere?" he persisted.

My jaw flexed, taking the lead on the irritation front and responding for the rest of my body. "Why would you say that?"

He sneered and pushed his glasses up higher. "It seems obvious. The disastrous premiere. Your injury. The layers of secrecy and security and whispered conversations."

"There's nothing to know," I insisted.

"Something's going on," he said. "This was no accident."

"It sounds like a nice conspiracy theory."

He stepped closer. "I heard there's a big secret fan club out there who insists on playing with you."

My cheeks warmed, and I stared at him, trying to read his body language. All I could see was the inelegance, though, and nothing else. "Where did you hear that?"

He shrugged, looking a little smug. "I have sources."

"Well, your sources are wrong."

"Are they wrong when they say they're feeding you clues about your father's disappearance? That they're trying to keep Raven Remington alive? I hear that people have traveled here from all over the country to meet together."

My stomach turned into ice. "What else do you know?"

The smirk returned. "You feed me information, and I'll feed you information. Deal?"

It was tempting. Very tempting. But I couldn't give up clues here. I'd already made my fair share of mistakes in every investigation I'd ever tried to help with. I wanted to prove myself worthy of this one by not ruining things.

"I need to go," I said.

Zane pushed past the man and unlocked my door. Then he helped me inside and slammed my door. I quickly locked it, just in case.

But I was feeling more and more unsettled by the moment.

CHAPTER TWENTY-FOUR

THIRTY MINUTES LATER, I was resting on a hammock and the breeze coming over the water from the Albemarle Sound gently swayed me back and forth.

Zane had made me my favorite smoothie—it had spinach and pineapple. He was recording various snippets for his blog and YouTube channel, capturing the quintessential beach life around us.

Zane's friend had his guitar out, and he played some beachy-sounding tunes in the background. Another friend played the bongos.

If it wasn't for the total chaos in my life, this would be perfect. More than perfect.

And, the good news was that Abe—Gerrard's friend—wasn't here yet, which gave me a few minutes to unwind.

Which was good because all I wanted to do right now was chill out—and that's exactly what I was doing.

Physically, at least.

My mind, on the other hand, was going a million miles a minute.

How had Awkward Reporter found out that information about my fan club? Who was his source?

Was he right? Was the production the target of this sabotage? Or was it me? Or Carli?

I let out a sigh.

I honestly had no idea.

Most of the time when I tried to be nosy, I had to hunt down the clues. But in this case, everyone seemed to be coming to me.

I wasn't sure if that was a good or bad thing.

But I'd take whatever answers I could get.

After thinking about it some more, I decided I did want to talk to Helena. She was a carnie. She'd know what it would take to pull off a stunt like this. Maybe she could give me some insight.

I also wanted to talk to the security guard and see if he'd seen anything. I was sure the police had already talked to him, but I wanted to hear what he had to say myself.

"How's it going down there?" Zane leaned his head down from his hammock above me.

Yes, it was a double-decker hammock, strung between two posts on the deck, and Zane was on top.

At first, I'd blanched at the idea. I mean, what if his hammock got loose and fell on me? I mean, if it happened to anyone, it could happen to me. But they'd seemed pretty tightly tied, so I'd decided to trust him.

"It's fine. It's nice. This is island living as I imagined it."

"Isn't it great? I could spend all day like this."

"It would be hard to pay the bills though." Even when you made millions, it didn't really matter. You always needed more.

"Can I get you anything?" Zane asked.

"No, this is perfect. Thanks for including me in this

little surfer club here. Now I know where you like to disappear to when you're not selling houses or doing massages or fixing surfboards."

"It's awesome. This is how life should be."

I closed my eyes and actually relaxed a moment.

And then Abe arrived.

———

Abe was all lean muscles, on the shorter side, and had tattoos covering every visible surface of his skin—except his face. His hair was graying and long and pulled into a ponytail, and apparently he'd run marathons, done Spartan types of races, and won triathlons.

Zane had told me that much.

As soon as there was a natural opening, Zane called him over.

"Abe, this is my friend Joey," Zane said.

"I've heard about you," he said. "Pleasure to meet you."

"You too."

We started with chitchat. I learned that Abe had lived in the area for fifteen years, and he was such an extrovert that I had a feeling he knew everyone. He was someone I needed to keep in mind because he seemed quite resourceful. And he didn't even seem to care that I was famous.

But, alas, I needed to get down to business.

"I hear you're friends with Gerrard," I started.

"Oh yeah. Gerrard. We like to surf together," he said, leaning against a fake totem pole. "He knows how to catch a good wave."

"He's apparently disappeared," I said. "Any idea where he is?"

He shrugged. "I can't say I keep tabs on him. Why do you want to know?"

His demeanor changed from relaxed to slightly on guard.

I decided to play it straight. "I heard he was arguing with my friend Carli on the day before her accident. I just want to find out why."

"You think he did this?"

I frowned, not liking where this was going. "I didn't say that. But I talked to him right after the accident while we were at the hospital. He never mentioned that to me."

"Just because he has a criminal record doesn't mean he's guilty."

"He has a criminal record?"

His gaze darkened. "It was just for some petty theft when he was younger," he said. "He learned his lesson and moved on."

I was definitely messing with the positive vibes of this party. Even the singer in the corner had switched to a mellow, sad tune about how life wasn't fair and we needed to stick it to the man.

"I'm not accusing anyone," I reiterated.

He leaned closer. "This is really what you want to know," he said. "His daughter was diagnosed with a rare genetic disorder three years ago. The local hospital couldn't help her."

"Okay . . ."

"He was bitter, but that doesn't mean he would target a hospital event. You'd think he'd want to help the hospital so they could bulk up their department."

Well, that was good to know. I hadn't expected him to share that. Not at all.

"I am just concerned because no one's been able to catch up with him."

"He'll make himself known when it's time," Abe said. "If he's not a suspect, then there's nothing to worry about." He winked. "Now, enjoy that smoothie."

———

Zane took me back to the house around dinnertime, and I felt like I'd wasted a lot of my day. But my body had needed the rest. Besides, I may not have been out actively trying to find answers, but my mind was reeling as I reviewed what I knew. That should count for something, right?

I'd formulated ways to find the security guard. On the drive back, I'd returned some emails from the mayor and Rutherford. Now that Carli was awake and okay, they were trying to reschedule the premiere in two days.

But if we didn't find out who was behind this, were we just setting ourselves up for another disaster? It was a possibility.

I needed to talk things over with Jackson.

But first I needed more medicine to relieve the ache in my foot. As I sat on my couch, trying to cool off, I reached into my purse to grab my prescription. As I rifled through the contents, I looked up at Zane.

"So I know this is none of my business, but did you have company last night?"

He sat down across from me. "Company?"

"I heard music. Saw a car."

"Oh." His face went slack. "It was nothing. Just an old friend who came back into town."

Interesting. He definitely seemed like he was being elusive. But why? I supposed it wasn't any of my business.

I looked through some makeup, some old receipts, and a spilled cylinder of gum. I still couldn't find my medicine. Finally, I dumped the contents of my purse onto the couch.

That confirmed it: my medicine was no longer in here.

That couldn't be right.

I tugged my bag into my lap and began digging through the deep recesses to see if it was stuck in one of the inner pockets.

Still nothing.

My pain medication wasn't there.

"What's wrong?" Zane asked.

I frowned. "I can't find my Vicodin."

"When did you take it last?"

"This morning."

He squinted. "Are you sure it was in your purse?"

I nodded, clearly remembering putting the bottle in there before I left. "I'm positive."

"What could have happened . . ." His face went from slack to struck with realization. "Wait, you don't think one of my friends took it, do you?"

"I didn't say that." Surfers did have a certain reputation, but I wasn't ready to point any fingers. Of course, he'd had some drug problems—pain relievers—when he was younger, after he'd been in a car accident.

I let out a mental sigh.

Zane stared at me, some of the friendliness gone from his eyes. "You didn't deny it."

"I'm still thinking this through, Zane. I do know that I left my purse on a chair at your friend's place, and I may have drifted off to sleep for a moment."

He adamantly swung his head back and forth. "My friends wouldn't do that. Where else did you leave your purse? There's got to be somewhere else someone could have taken that medicine."

I tried to think it through, to remember each moment from today. So much had happened. "I had it with me at the hospital. I mean, I think I set it down once when I was talking to people in the waiting room."

"It could have been anyone there then."

I rubbed my lips together, trying to carefully choose my words in order to promote peace instead of strife. "Zane, it's like I said—I'm not accusing. I just realized my pain reliever was missing, and I'm trying to figure this out."

I stared at him, wondering why he'd reacted so strongly so quickly. There was more to this story.

He raked a hand through his hair, still not looking convinced. "I get it. Can I get you something else? Some over-the-counter pain reliever?"

I nodded. "That would be great."

I leaned back, giving myself a moment to breathe now that Zane had walked away.

That hadn't played out very well.

And the fact that narcotics had gone missing from my person didn't make me feel better either. The last thing I wanted to do was feed this country's drug epidemic.

I let out another mental sigh. Why couldn't life ever be easy and simple?

Zane returned, and I took two tablets.

I couldn't wait until my foot healed. It was causing so many issues in my life right now. And it was slowing me down when I didn't want to be slowed down.

I closed my eyes, trying to collect my thoughts, but before I could really start, someone knocked at the door. Zane pulled it open and revealed Jackson standing on the other side.

He must be coming to take over babysitting duty.

But when he stepped inside and I saw his eyes, I knew there was more to it.

"Joey, have you seen Rutherford or talked to him lately?"

Rutherford? I shook my head. "No, not since I was at the hospital earlier. Why?"

Something was wrong. Jackson wouldn't have stopped by to ask me this personally otherwise.

"He's missing," Jackson announced. "No one has seen him for hours."

There had to be a logical explanation for this.

"Maybe he left." I tried to review the messages he'd sent me. Had he indicated he was leaving? No, he hadn't.

"All his bags are still at his house," Jackson said. "He's not answering his cell. And he missed an appointment with the press."

"He missed an appointment? With the press? You're right. That doesn't sound like him." My concern swelled until it felt like a rock had settled in my heart.

Jackson's uneasy gaze latched on to mine. "We think this might be connected with everything that's been going on, Joey. Until we know for sure, promise me that you'll be careful. Very careful."

Fear rippled through me. "I will. I promise."

CHAPTER TWENTY-FIVE

I HUNG UP MY PHONE. I'd called everyone I could possibly think of to ask about Rutherford, and no one had seen him.

His last known location was at his beach house, where he'd gone to freshen up before more meetings. He was supposed to have met with none other than Burly Reporter man at two, but Rutherford hadn't shown up.

What had happened between his lunch appointment with the mayor, going to freshen up, and his meeting with the reporter?

I didn't know, but I didn't like any of this.

And why did my foot have to hurt so badly?

I couldn't let something as minor as a sprained ankle and stitches slow me down. They wouldn't deter Chuck Norris. So for that reason, I called Mayor Allen.

"I'm sorry to hear about your manager," he said. "I'm hoping this is all a big misunderstanding. Rutherford seems like an amazing young man who's brought so many wonderful ideas to the table."

It was hard to take him seriously with his lisp. "I'm glad

he's been helpful. Did he say anything strange to you during your lunch?"

"I can't say he did. We talked about the premiere we were rescheduling. What we'd do different. How to get the word out."

"Did he seem upset or distracted?"

"No, he seemed just fine. If something was wrong, I had no clue. Sorry I can't be more help."

But actually, he could. "Mayor, I'd like to get in touch with the security guard you hired for the backstage area. Could you give me his name?"

"I'll transfer you to my assistant. She'll have that information."

A moment later, Lori was on the phone. "Hey, Joey. You need a name?"

"The security guard, please."

"That's Matt Myers. He works events around here on occasion. Sometimes he's a bouncer at some clubs. He tried to become a cop, but it didn't work out for him. That's what my mom told me one time, at least. They're both members of the Loyal Order of the Beaver."

Interesting. "Any idea where I can find him now?"

"If I had to guess? The gun range. He practically lives there."

The shooting range?

My stomach sank.

That was so not the place I wanted to talk to anyone about this case. But a girl had to do what a girl had to do.

———

I convinced Zane to take me to the gun range. He was still in a funk, which concerned me. Did he know something that he wasn't telling me? I couldn't read him. Despite that, I had to press on.

The gun range that Matt Myers liked to frequent was located across the water in an area known as Mann's Harbor. Zane told me that the area was known for their large black bear population and the Alligator River National Wildlife Refuge.

Yes, there were apparently alligators living only thirty minutes from where I was.

That wasn't extremely comforting.

At the entrance to the range, Zane and I showed our ID, paid a fee, and were given a brief introductory course. Then we picked out pistols, paid for some ammunition, and made our way over to a line of people who were practicing to hit their targets.

Sure enough, Matt Myers was here looking all *Lone Survivor* with his assault rifle.

I had to come up with a plan. Plans weren't my strength, however. But if I pretended to be Raven Remington, maybe I could think of a solution.

"Zane, we need to divide and conquer," I whispered, glancing around the massive gun range, which was full of trigger-happy men and women.

"What do you mean?"

"I need you to befriend Matt Myers." I nodded toward the man as another round of bullets expelled at a rapid fire from his gun.

"Why would I do that?" He looked slightly stupefied and mostly still annoyed.

"Because he'll recognize me."

He let out a small breath. "So what do I do?"

"Do your extrovert thing. Strike up a conversation. Get him talking, and bring the subject around to the movie premiere."

He still looked skeptical. "And what will you be doing?"

"Lingering close enough to hear." I balanced on one crutch and raised a hand in an innocent gesture.

"Don't point that thing at me!" Zane lowered my gun until the barrel pointed to the ground.

I quickly looked around to make sure I wasn't making a spectacle of myself. Everyone appeared busy putting bullets into the paper silhouettes of men in the distance. "Sorry. I don't know what I'm doing. The good news is that it's not loaded yet."

"I figured you would know basic gun safety," Zane said.

"Why would you think that?"

"Because you're . . ."

"Don't even say because I'm Raven Remington," I warned. I started to raise my gun again but stopped myself.

He shrugged, still not in good spirits. I wasn't used to Zane not being in good spirits.

"But you are Raven Remington. Kind of."

"I didn't need to know all the logistics of these things when I was acting like an expert. I just did what people said."

"Well, I'm not a fan of guns myself. Is this really the only way you could think of to do this?"

"Yes," I answered.

I liked fun Zane better than grumpy Zane. Had I mentioned that yet?

Before he could argue anymore, I did as any good amateur detective would do. I hobbled that way and took my place behind the little boothy-stally thingy two sections from Matt Myers. I set my gun on a ledge there and balanced on my uninjured ankle.

"So?" I whispered to Zane, subtly nodding toward Matt.

He scowled. "I'm not promising I'm going to shoot this thing. But I will try to strike up a conversation."

"How hard can it be?" Propping my hip up against the edge, I picked up my gun again. And, again, I accidentally aimed the barrel at Zane. I quickly corrected myself, but not before Zane saw me.

"That sounds like something someone says before they accidentally maim themselves—or the person beside them."

I had to be careful since there was a good chance Matt was going to recognize me. I had donned a ball cap and some old reading glasses, so there was nothing glamorous about my appearance now. And he seemed pretty focused on shooting his little gun/rifle/pistol-ma-gadget.

If I thought about it long enough, I could remember some of the sidearm names. But I didn't want to. I needed to save all my thinking cells to find this bad guy.

I made sure that the sides of my booth were mostly concealing me. And since Zane was doing the whole man-bun look today coupled with a headband and a scowl, he might not be recognizable either. I hoped. Plus, his aura was totally off.

Seriously, I should be the one who was cranky. My drugs were missing.

Zane took his place on the opposite side of Matt Myers. Another man stood between us, a man who'd been talking to Matt Myers. Were they friends? Maybe.

I fiddled with my gun for a few minutes, loading the bullets into the magazine and pretending like I was lining up to shoot my target.

A conversation between Matt Myers and Zane caught my ear and pulled me from my strangled thoughts about my neighbor. I tried to listen between the rounds of gunfire around me, but the protective ear gear I'd been given made it difficult. I loosened the plugs.

"I'll tell you what—those Hollywood types?" Matt aimed his gun at a target. "They don't deserve to make millions. The real heroes are the police officers. The cops. The paramedics. The soldiers."

I totally agreed with him. I hadn't picked the amount my profession paid. Or football players. Or other athletes or celebrities. For that matter, most in my profession suffered with feast or famine. A lot of famine.

"I agree," Zane said.

"It makes me so mad." Matt squeezed the trigger.

The loud pop made me nearly jump out of my skin.

"I've busted my butt for years trying to do right. I don't even get a thank-you. Meanwhile, those talentless people get treated like they're saviors of the world. Most of them are just messed up."

"You're right," Zane said. "It doesn't sound fair."

"I worked at that premiere this week," he said. "The one where the actress nearly died."

"That was some messed-up stuff."

"She got what she had coming to her," Matt mumbled. "That's all I can say."

My heart stuttered in my chest.

Got what she had coming?

He sounded like a suspect if you asked me.

———

I decided I didn't really want to shoot my gun. Instead, I leaned across my boothy-stally thing toward the man Matt Myers had been speaking with when we arrived. The man, who I'd guessed to be in his sixties, was reloading his gun.

Questioning people who are holding guns had to be the worst idea ever.

I could add it to my list of unwise things I'd done in my life. Marrying Eric was right at the top.

"You look like you know what you're doing." I nodded toward his gun, trying to sound super impressed and not like someone who'd pretended to be a sharpshooter in my past fictional life.

He shrugged and clicked his magazine in place. "I like to think that. Former military, member of the NRA, and avid hunter. Your first time?"

I nodded. "I'm trying to mark it off my bucket list. I figure every single girl should know how to protect herself."

"I see. Well, there are a lot of people here who can help, if you need it."

"Good to know."

As soon as I said that, Matt's voice rose above everyone else's. "Society. It's messed up," he continued. "Plain and simple. Our priorities are all out of whack."

I glanced at the man beside me, and he shook his head, looking like he'd heard this spiel a million times before. "Pay no attention to him. He's got opinions about everything from how to grow tomatoes to what he would do if he was POTUS."

"Sounds like it. I heard him talking about the woes of the rich and famous earlier." I did a half eye roll.

He let out a sigh and glanced at his target down the lane. "That's a daily tirade."

Interesting. "Is it really?"

"Yeah. I'm not sure what kind of change he hopes to accomplish by spouting out about it so much," he said, still not looking at me. "Telling people here how things need to change will do little to change things. I told him that a couple of weeks ago, and he said he had an idea."

My heart stuttered again. "Did he? I wonder what it was."

"No clue, but he seemed pretty excited about it. Said it would open people's eyes. After all, the problem isn't Hollywood or celebrities. It's the fact that society allows undeserved treatment and respect to happen."

This security guy was looking more and more like he could be behind everything that happened.

"Anyway," the man continued. "I'm sure that's more than you wanted to hear. You came here to shoot a gun, not listen to an old man ramble."

"No, it was very interesting."

A touch of satisfaction filled me. I'd just successfully found out information without tipping anyone off.

I was getting better at this detective thing all the time.

Raven Remington would be proud.

Just then, I heard Matt's loud voice across the range. "Hey, aren't you that actress?"

Okay, maybe I *wasn't* that great at this detective thing.

I sighed.

But my sigh quickly faded when I saw Matt's gun aimed at me.

CHAPTER TWENTY-SIX

MY THROAT TIGHTENED as Matt stormed toward me, gun in his hand.

My friend—the unnamed one I'd just made—stood between us.

Guns. Questioning people at a gun range. Had I mentioned just how horrible that idea was? It was really horrible. Really, really horrible.

Especially the fact that I was questioning an angry man at the gun range.

Matt glared at me. "What are you doing here, Little Miss Walk of Fame?"

I'd never been called that before. "I'm free to shoot a gun, aren't I?"

He narrowed his eyes. "Did you follow me?"

"Who are you?" I asked, trying to play dumb. "And why would I follow you?"

"You don't even recognize me? You Hollywood types." He swung his head back and forth with contempt. "You think you're so much better than everyone else. Overpaid. Presumptuous. Out of touch."

"I don't know what you're talking about." I raised my chin. He sounded like the king of generalizations, if you asked me.

"Again—out of touch." He sneered.

I decided to go with a different tactic. "Hey, I do recognize you. Aren't you that security guard?"

His eyes lit, and he spit beside him before turning to address me again. "What do you know? The little princess does recognize the little people in her life."

The man was bitter. Really bitter. It was like I'd personally wronged him, even though I'd never spoken to the man other than to add Jackson and Zane to the *approved* list.

"You were there the night of the accident and bomb threat, right?" I asked, trying to feel him out.

His gaze darkened. "What about it?"

"Did you see anything suspicious that night?"

"The police have already talked to me," he said. "I have nothing more to say."

He definitely seemed squirrelly, like he could be hiding something. But what? And how did I figure that out? I supposed I'd go with asking directly.

"You sound like someone who might want to ruin a movie premiere," I ventured, knowing I'd probably regret it.

He was holding a gun, after all.

The man leered at me. "You don't know nothing about me."

Well, now, that wasn't exactly true.

"I know you hate me and you don't even know me," I said.

"You're an entitled little brat."

"You're making assumptions, and I'm sensing you're very unhappy with your life."

Raven had tried to make nice and use psychology like

that sometimes. It was the only thing I could pull out of my bag of tricks.

"My son died in Iraq. He barely made enough to live on. And you pretend to be someone else and get paid millions."

My heart pounded in my ears.

The man had a point.

Compassion replaced my suspicions—though he wasn't totally off my suspect list. Grief could do horrible things to people.

"I'm sorry," I said. "That's wrong."

He opened his mouth like he might argue but stopped himself. "It sure is."

Zane tugged my arm. "We should go."

I agreed.

But as Matt Myers limped away, I realized he would have had a hard time climbing that scaffolding.

———

I was kind of grumpy with Zane when we got back to my place. I knew he'd insist on staying with me—he'd promised Jackson that he would—so I didn't bother to argue.

Instead, I excused myself and headed up to my room, feigning exhaustion. I tried to put some weight on my foot, and it didn't feel too bad, so I forced myself to walk up the stairs by myself, even though Zane had offered to help.

Maybe I was being too grumpy with him, but I couldn't help it.

I bypassed my room and went into one of the spare bedrooms. In the closet there, I'd set up my own little police station. I kept all the clues that I'd discovered about my dad since he disappeared last year.

I'd put together a timeline of his last days. I'd talked to people who interacted with him. I'd tried to find out as much information as possible.

And I still had no great leads.

My dad was the whole reason I'd come here. Our last conversation had been terse, and I couldn't let things end on that note. And it wasn't like my dad to walk away without a single word. That was why I knew something was wrong.

I sat on a little bean bag chair I'd set up in here and stared at all the information.

I stared at my dad's picture. At his warm eyes that portrayed his quiet demeanor and steadfast faithfulness. I missed him so much. He'd always been there for me, and I was faltering without his guidance.

What would you tell me now, Dad?

I looked up at the ceiling, as if the answer would come down from above.

He would tell me to live my life with integrity. But what did that look like in everyday life? In this situation specifically?

I wasn't sure.

I just knew that I wanted the person responsible for this to come to justice. I'd promised my help—however floundering it might be.

I closed my eyes now and thought about my future. Where would I be next year at this time? Could I still see myself staying here? Could I be an actress and live in this area?

I wasn't sure.

I was getting a lot of calls from people—producers—who were interested in casting me in new movies. Some of the names were big. Some could do great things as far as cementing my career and ensuring future success.

But I had to figure out my priorities first.

And that was where that good old-fashioned integrity came in again.

Integrity certainly didn't mean stringing two guys along and then leaving them both.

I sighed. I was going to have to take this day by day. Because when I looked at the big picture, all I felt was overwhelmed.

That's what you should do, Joey. Figure out this case. Find your dad. And by then more answers should come to light.

———

Zane was in better spirits the next morning, and he handed me a smoothie. I sat at the breakfast bar, drank it, and listened to him jabber on about the waves outside. He obviously wanted to go surfing, and I didn't want to be the one who stopped him from catching the big one.

It would all work out, however, because Jackson had texted me and let me know Zane was being relieved of duty and he was in charge of me today instead.

Also to my surprise, Zane didn't argue about it.

What was going on?

Zane set his glass down and rested his elbows on the breakfast bar. He had a strange look in his eyes as he gazed at me.

"Let's get lost," Zane said.

I let out a laugh—until I realized he was serious. Then I set down my smoothie and stared back at him. "What do you mean?"

His gaze locked on mine. "What's holding us back? Let's get out of here. Take off. Go somewhere. Anywhere."

"Why would we do that?" This was like the *Field of Dreams* popping up overnight or something. Where had it come from? Out of left field, that was where.

"Because we can. Because life is short. Because . . . well, just because." He shrugged.

My heart pounded in my ears. The idea was tempting. Very tempting.

Leaving everything behind. Forgetting my worries. Pretending my problems didn't exist.

But I knew I couldn't do that.

The truth was, I was already lost. I'd come here to find my dad, and that was exactly what I intended on doing, even if it took me years.

No more running away from my problems or reality.

No matter how enticing.

"Zane, I can't," I said softly.

He frowned and looked down at the counter. "I kind of thought you might say that."

"Are you going to get lost without me?"

He shrugged, shifting his gaze to the window—to the waves. "I don't know. I feel like I just need to clear my head."

Was he facing some kind of personal crisis? That was what it sounded like. But he didn't seem to want to open up to me about it. Maybe he would in his own time.

"I get that."

He straightened. "Let me get cleaned up in here."

"Good idea. I need to grab something from my purse."

I tottered toward my purse so I could grab my favorite lip gloss—Downtown Fig. As I passed by Zane's overnight bag, which was stashed near the entrance, something caught my eye. Panic swept through me.

It couldn't be.

But I had to be certain.

I glanced behind me. Zane still whistled in the kitchen.

My throat clenched as I turned back toward his bag and crept closer.

My assumptions had to be wrong.

But I needed to know for sure.

Still listening to Zane whistle, I leaned toward his bag, knowing good and well that this was an invasion of privacy.

I picked up the brownish-orange container peeking from the edges and sucked in a breath.

It was pain pills. My pain pills.

Zane had taken them? Why would he have done that? And he'd lied about it.

"What are you doing?" a deep voice said.

I nearly jumped out of my skin.

I looked up and saw Zane staring at me.

CHAPTER TWENTY-SEVEN

"YOU HAVE MY PILLS," I muttered, showing him the bottle.

His lips parted with surprise. "I have no idea how those got there."

"Zane . . ." I didn't want to accuse him, but all the evidence was stacked against him right now.

"You really think I took those, Joey?"

I heard the tension in his voice and knew I needed to handle this with care. "How else did they get here?"

His hands went to his hips. "Someone planted them."

I'd been accused of being naïve and gullible before, and I hated being lumped into that category. "You didn't pack this bag until you got home. Has anyone seen you since then?"

He scowled. "I don't know. But I didn't put them there. I thought you were my friend, Joey."

"I am your friend, and that's why I'm concerned." Drug addicts didn't always tell the truth. And I knew he'd had a problem with pain killers in the past. I couldn't pretend this hadn't happened.

"You need to believe me." His eyes were pleading.

I counted my pills. If my estimates were correct, I was missing four. I slipped the bottle into my pocket, unsure what to think. I wanted to believe him. I did.

We'd had some crazy stuff happen to us together. Was this just one more crazy thing to add to that list? Possibly.

We stared at each other, and I knew I needed to make a choice. "I'm going to trust that you're not lying to me. But how did this bottle get into the bag?"

"I have no idea, but I'll try to find out." An awkward moment of silence passed between us, and finally Zane glanced at his watch. "Do you know when Jackson will be here?"

I shrugged. "Anytime now."

He snatched his bag and stepped to the door. "I'm going to go get changed then. You'll be okay a few minutes by yourself?"

"I'm sure I will be." Actually, I wasn't sure, not with my luck. But having some space from Zane seemed like a great idea right now.

He opened the door and stepped out. But before he left, he paused. "Are you going to tell Jackson about this?"

My throat went dry. Was I? That was a good question. I wasn't sure what I was going to do. "I don't know."

His gaze darkened. "I thought you believed me."

"Someone stole my prescription pain killers. It's a big deal."

He gave me one last glance before leaving. I closed the door and leaned back, feeling rotten.

If I were in Zane's shoes, I'd want to be given the benefit of the doubt.

I felt like an awful person. And I hated feeling like an awful person.

I might as well be.

Someone knocked at the door again, and I hoped it was Zane coming back to explain. I hated ending things on a rotten note.

I pulled the door open. Jackson stood there.

He didn't look any happier than I felt.

Great . . . what now? My day had already been full of so much sunshine.

"The chief has requested you come down to the station," he said.

My entire body tensed with panic. "Why? What happened?"

"There was a shooting last night. Your prints were found on the gun."

———

Certainly I hadn't heard Jackson correctly. "What do you mean my prints were found on a gun?"

He dropped his head to the side and frowned apologetically. "Exactly what it sounds like."

"I don't even own a gun."

"I didn't say you owned it. I said your prints were on it."

I sucked in a breath as realization washed over me. "The shooting range."

Jackson raised an eyebrow. "The shooting range?"

I nodded. "I was there yesterday, and I held a gun."

"What in the world were you doing there yesterday?" That familiar flabbergasted tone entered his voice.

"That's where I talked to Matt Myers." Duh.

Jackson stared me down. "You went to a gun range to talk to a suspect? Please tell me he wasn't practicing at the time."

I squirmed, which was apparently enough of an answer for Jackson. When he said it that way, it sounded so bad.

"Joey . . ."

I shrugged. "I had a lapse of judgment."

I waited for him to tell me I had a lot of those, but he didn't.

Maybe my whole life was a lapse of judgment. My career. My choice in a spouse. Figuring out my love life now. I was having trouble getting things right.

Jackson lowered his gaze and his voice, almost like he could sense my inner turmoil. "We still have to take you in. You'll at least need to sign a statement."

"How did you even match my fingerprints?" Did the police have some kind of secret file on me?

"We took them to rule you out that time when you contaminated the crime scene of that dead man."

"Which one?" Did I honestly have to ask that?

"Words I never want to hear." He shook his head. "The man you found at the hotel. The one you puked on."

My mouth formed an O. "That one."

He cast me a knowing glance. "Let's get this over with."

I glanced at my watch. "I have a doctor's appointment in two hours. Do I need to cancel?"

"No, I'll make sure you get there."

CHAPTER TWENTY-EIGHT

TWO HOURS LATER, I sat in the waiting room at the doctor's office. I'd called yesterday in between everything else, and Jackson's doctor had been able to squeeze me in today.

Jackson sat beside me. I wasn't sure if he felt like a warden, a bodyguard, or a babysitter. At different times, he felt like each, I supposed.

At the police station, I'd discovered that someone had shot out the windows in the trailer I'd been using as my dressing room and backstage area. No one had been hurt. That was the good news.

The bad news was that someone had stolen that gun from the range and tried to set me up. That would mean that someone had followed me. Kept an eye on the gun I used. Somehow stole it. All the while, I hadn't noticed a thing. Maybe a keen power of observation wasn't my strength.

Had I been set up the same way someone had possibly set up Eric as the one who'd left those broken bottles?

The same way that someone had potentially planted my pain pills on Zane?

Should I mention those pain pills to Jackson?

Again, my emotions warred inside me. I didn't know what to do. I didn't want to make my friend look bad if he was innocent. I mean, friends didn't accuse friends of things they didn't do.

I decided to remain quiet, and I hoped I didn't regret it.

But I regretted so much that there was a good chance I'd regret this also.

A girl stopped by and asked for my autograph. She wore bright-blue eyeshadow all the way up to her eyebrows. I bit back a smile.

When she left, my gaze was drawn to a TV in the corner as the morning news scrolled across the screen. Eric's picture filled the tube, causing me to pause. Why was he on TV?

I got up and moved closer. I wanted to hear. Yet I didn't.

"Eric Lauderdale has been awarded the prestigious Golden Apple Award for his charity work," the reporter said. "This humanitarian award is considered one of the highest honors someone can receive. Lauderdale has worked tirelessly to help people suffering with life-threatening illnesses."

Pictures flashed across the screen. Pictures of Eric with people in hospital gowns. They smiled at the camera. Gave a thumbs-up. Eric kissed an older lady on the cheek.

All the photos looked heartwarming and kind, like he was such an upstanding citizen.

I remembered his volunteer work for those charities. He'd grumbled about how demanding the people were. How he was only doing it because it would look good on his résumé. How he really just wanted to act, and how he resented having to do other things all for the sake of public image.

Nothing about him was sincere, but he was a great actor. He could put on a great show and make people believe he was a good guy.

A hand on my shoulder brought me back to the present. "You okay?"

I knew it was Jackson.

I nodded, pushing the images I'd just seen out of my mind. Trying to, at least. "I guess so."

"He'll get what's coming to him one day," Jackson said.

"Maybe," I muttered.

I remembered Eric's warning to me. If I talked about him, then he would press charges against Jackson. I knew Jackson would say he didn't care. But I cared. I couldn't let this ruin Jackson's career—or just plain ruin Jackson.

"What he did to you was wrong," Jackson continued.

"It's my word against his word at this point."

"He's going to continue the cycle."

His words caused my gut to twist. How could I protect everyone? I knew the answer—I couldn't.

"Ms. Darling?" a nurse called at that moment.

"That's me," I said, my voice catching.

I pushed myself to my feet and went back to the examination room.

Over the next twenty minutes, the doctor told me that my ankle was healing and that there were no signs of infection in my cuts. That was the good news. As soon as I felt comfortable enough to walk without crutches, I could do it. That was also good news. Then he encouraged me to stay off my ankle as much as possible.

That was the bad news.

"Do you need more pain medication?" The doctor closed my chart as we wrapped up.

I remembered those pills in Zane's stuff. I wanted to stay as far away from narcotics as possible.

"No," I told him. "Some extra-strength over-the-counter stuff should be just fine."

As he left and I gathered my purse, my phone buzzed. Despite not recognizing the number, I saw it was local and answered.

"Joey?" a woman said. "I can't believe you answered."

I couldn't believe I answered either. What had I been thinking? "Who is this?"

"It's Helena."

Helena. I definitely shouldn't have answered. But since I had, I continued with, "What's going on?"

"Listen, could you meet for coffee?" she asked. "I have something important to talk to you about. It concerns Carli."

My pulse spiked. "Of course."

———

I shifted in my chair at the coffeehouse. It was one of my favorite places here in the Outer Banks—Sunrise Coffee Co. It was eclectic, local, and tasty.

Actually, I also enjoyed Oh Buoy, a smoothie bar. And Fatty Shack, a seafood restaurant. There were so many places in this area with fresh, tasty food. Which was why I tried to stick with raw food. Except when I didn't.

Just the smell of coffee and vanilla . . . the sound of whip cream bursting to life, mingling with the tones of Ed Sheeran made me feel like everything was right in the world.

"My screenplay needs to be made into a movie," Helena stated.

I stared at her. "This was the important thing we needed to talk about?"

Helena nodded from across the table, where she sipped her espresso. "What did you think it was about?"

"Carli."

She shrugged. "Why would I know about Carli?"

I tried to hold my irritation at bay, but it wanted to come ashore and release its inner rage. Yes, my irritation had an inner rage. Stop judging.

"Because you're her friend."

"*Friend* would be an exaggeration. We hardly liked each other as teens."

"But you spoke about her at the vigil. And you said you were practically BFFs."

"Of course I did. It was the right thing. We go way back." She stared at me with crazy eyes and parted lips.

"You said you wanted to meet me concerning Carli," I reminded her.

"Once I get someone to produce my play, I'll give some proceeds to her medical care."

"You are one very confusing person, Helena." And I thought I was bad.

"Can we keep talking about my screenplay? It was inspired by the last man who dumped me. There are a lot of them. I always thought I'd be married by now . . ."

"Is that right?" My words were lackluster, to say the least.

"I thought I was going to marry Mike. But he ended up being a jerk. Nothing like the guys in the movies. Can you give me some tips on how to meet that kind of life mate?"

"Uh . . ." Did she think movie heroes were real?

"But it doesn't matter," she continued. "Romance is so yesterday. Today, it's all about my screenplay . . ."

I tried to tune her out. I just couldn't handle this right now. I had too many other things going on in my life to deal with someone who was obviously out of touch with reality.

I glanced at Jackson. He sat at another table with his hat pulled down low and his newspaper raised. I'd told him it was better if he wasn't there, because Helena was more likely to open up.

But he edged the paper down low enough that I could see the sparkle in his eyes.

I had to be the most unintuitive person ever. The worst detective ever. I'd really thought Helena had information. Enough so that Jackson was taking time from his investigation to allow me to talk to her.

At least he still had his humor about him, because I could easily justify any irritation on his part.

I was irritated myself.

"So what do you say?" Helena blinked as if she honestly thought I might help her break away from her life as a carnie.

"I don't know what to say, Helena."

"Can you take this?" She shoved the manuscript toward me.

Was Jackson really sure that this girl had an alibi for the evening of the movie premiere? Because I almost wanted her to be guilty.

They weren't my kindest thoughts, but I was having a rough day, and it wasn't even lunchtime yet.

I read the manuscript title out loud. "I Hate You."

That sounded like a winner.

How was I going to gracefully get myself out of this one?

Her gaze shifted, and she leaned toward me. Her entire demeanor changed from excited to engaged. "You agree to read it, and I'll tell you something I know."

And here we went again. I had to clarify her statement before I agreed to anything. "Is it something pertaining to this investigation?"

"Of course." She snorted again, like I was stupid.

"Okay, what is it?"

A gleam filled her eyes. "Tim and Carli have been arguing."

Now she had my attention. It was the first I'd heard of this. "What do you mean?"

"It's a well-known fact in carnie circles. Tim wants Carli to give up being a stuntwoman."

"Why would he want that?" I glanced at Jackson. His attention was on this conversation.

"Because he wants to have kids."

"So you think he staged this to ensure she'd have to leave this career behind?" It seemed a little extreme.

"I'm not saying anything. I'm just letting you know what I heard on the carnie scene. Her parents and my parents are still friends, you know. If you haven't looked into him, you should."

"Thanks, Helena."

She pushed her papers closer to me. "Let me know what you think about my screenplay."

CHAPTER TWENTY-NINE

JACKSON TOOK me to see Carli at the hospital after we left Sunrise.

He'd heard what Helena told me, and he was going to talk to Tim as I talked to Carli.

Tim was in the waiting room. He'd been by Carli's side ever since this happened. The two truly seemed to have a great relationship. But Helena's words haunted me. I hoped he wasn't guilty. I really hoped.

I was buzzed in to see Carli. When I walked into her room, she didn't see me initially. I quickly observed how she was still hooked up to numerous machines. Most of her body was bandaged. But her color looked better.

"Hey." Carli smiled at me, still not moving her head. "Any updates on the case?"

I wondered if anyone had told her that Rutherford was missing. I wasn't sure. Maybe news like that wouldn't help her recovery. It was so hard to know.

I did know that Carli was a strong lady. One of the strongest I knew.

"The police are still searching for answers," I said.

"Carli, did you have any encounters with a security guard named Matt before you went on?"

She seemed to think about it a moment before shaking her head. "I do vaguely remember a security guard being back there. He kept watching me during rehearsal, and it was almost freaky."

"But you didn't see him near your harness?"

She shook her head. "No, I'm sorry. I wish I'd seen more."

"There were a few reporters around," I continued. "Did any of them give you a hard time?"

"I can't say they did," she said. "Most people don't want to interview me though. They want to interview you."

"So you think someone else may have been the target?" I asked. And by someone else, I meant me.

She shrugged. "It's hard to say. But only a handful of us knew that I was the one in that harness and not you. Do you remember at practice we actually put you in the harness, Joey?"

I nodded. We'd been goofing off and just trying to have fun. Fun was the one thing I was good at.

"The more I think about it, the more I'm convinced this was about you, Joey."

Carli's words hung in the air.

Maybe she was right.

But then why had Rutherford been snatched?

I shifted, knowing this conversation may not turn out to be pleasant. But I needed to have it. "Carli, Helena said that you and Tim have been arguing a lot lately. Is that true?"

Her face seemed to go pale. "Most married couples argue."

"You don't think . . ." I mean, Tim was the stunt coordinator. He was in the perfect position to do something like this. But I couldn't bring myself to say the words aloud.

"No. Absolutely not. Tim would never do this. Besides, we were together from after the rehearsal until the movie premiere started."

"I understand," I said. "Thank you. I just had to ask."

"I get that." She paused. "Listen, you know that Gerrard guy? The one I got into the argument with at the restaurant?"

"Yes?"

"I vaguely recall him sneaking behind the trailer while we were eating," she said. "I guess the medicine is messing with my brain. But I remembered that last night. Maybe it's nothing. But maybe it's something."

I'd take anything I could get at this point.

———

"So what did Tim say?" I asked as Jackson and I got into his car.

"He doesn't deny the fact that he wishes Carli would get out of the business," Jackson said. "But he said he would never injure her to assure that."

"That's what Carli said also. I believe them. I just can't see him taking it that far."

"You'd be surprise at how far some people would take it."

I glanced at him. "You looked into him before, right? The husband is always the first person you look at?"

He nodded. "We did, but he's got a clean record. We have no reason to suspect him."

"I really hope it wasn't him."

Jackson cranked the engine. "Listen, the guys want me

to stop by the festival site to see something," Jackson said once we were back in his car. "Are you up for it?"

"Sure thing."

"Okay. Because you look exhausted."

I wanted to tell him about Zane. It was weighing on my mind. But then I felt like I was betraying Zane.

Then again, Zane had been acting erratically lately.

Speaking of which . . . I squinted at a cluster of people in the distance.

Billy . . . and Zane.

"What are those two doing together?" Jackson asked.

The two of them stood on the corner, like they were about to cross the highway.

Billy owned a bar in town, and he was also shady. Very shady. But his dad was one of the wealthiest men in the area, so he always managed to slip by in investigations.

I didn't like the man. I wondered if he had something to do with my dad's disappearance . . . or at least if he knew about it.

"Who's the third guy?" Jackson asked.

I recognized the man from that day when my pills had been stolen. "His name is Abe."

"Why do you look so irritated?"

"Because someone took my Vicodin," I blurted.

I was never good at keeping secrets, and that one had just been begging to escape.

"What?" His voice was tinged with emotion. Anger? Irritation? Surprise? Maybe all three.

I nodded and explained what had happened.

"Why are you just telling me this now?" Jackson asked. "You should have come to me when it happened."

I shrugged. "I don't know. I want to believe the best in people. In friends."

Jackson let out a slow breath. "Zane used to be a drug addict."

"I know. But he's been clean for a while now." Yes, I was defending Zane. He would have defended me . . . right? This whole situation was so confusing.

"Well, if he's hanging out with Billy, then he's obviously not using good judgment right now."

I raked a hand through my hair. He had a point. "I don't know."

"You should file a report."

"Give me more time to get to the bottom of this first," I said. "I can handle this."

Said like a person who couldn't handle it.

When we arrived at the festival site, I was still feeling overwhelmed.

"Wait here. I'll be back," Jackson said.

I nodded. Normally, I'd want to tag along. I'd want to know what the other officers had found that Jackson might need to see—especially if it pertained to the investigation.

But my foot was throbbing. My head was throbbing. My ego had long ago deflated.

And in the middle of it all, I had to go to the bathroom.

I stared at the Porta-Potties across the field.

I hated Porta-Potties. But there was nothing else around. And I really had to go.

I glanced over to where Jackson was. I could probably slip away and be back before he ever noticed I was gone.

Besides, I didn't want to interrupt him for something this menial. There was no one else over there, so the chance that something would go wrong was slim to none.

That decided it.

I staggered up and decided to leave my crutches in the

car. I was going to attempt to walk across the field without them.

It took a few minutes, but I did it. I reached the row of portable bathrooms.

I opened the first one, and it was disgusting. Toilet paper was everywhere, the seat was wet, and the stench was awful.

I hobbled to the second one instead. It looked better . . . I thought. It still smelled horrible, but didn't they all?

I just needed to get this over with.

Holding my breath, I stepped inside and locked the door.

As a last-minute thought, I quickly pulled out my phone and texted Jackson what I was doing. I didn't want to face his questioning if he got back to the car in the five minutes I was gone.

Just as I put my phone away, I heard a strange noise outside.

What was that?

Then I recognized it. Tires screeching across asphalt. Probably in the parking lot on the other side of the field.

But close.

Too close for comfort.

My fingers fumbled with the door lock. I needed to check out what was going on, just in case it in any way pertained to me.

Before I could get the door unlatched, the whole Porta-Potty shifted.

It wobbled. Tilted. Rocked.

I grabbed the wall. The filthy wall.

Just as I did, the whole container crashed to the ground . . . and something wet and gooey and stinky covered me.

CHAPTER THIRTY

"JOEY!" someone yelled outside.

I could barely comprehend what was happening. The world flipped around me until I didn't know which end was up. I slammed into plastic. My shoulder. My knee. My other shoulder.

A car radio blared outside.

Finally, everything stopped.

I took in a deep breath and forced my eyes open. Aqua green surrounded me.

The next thing I knew, the whole place turned again.

It had landed on the door, I realized.

I slid at the gentle flip of the structure.

Then the door was flung open. Jackson and two of his officers stood there.

The concern on their faces quickly turned to disgust. Except for Jackson. He kept it professional as he reached for me. "Are you okay?"

He helped me onto the grass.

My bones all felt intact. And I hadn't started going to

the bathroom yet. That was good news because that would be really embarrassing.

But when I looked down, I realized I was covered in sewage.

From head to toe.

And I smelled like it also. Nausea roiled in me.

I touched my head and extracted a clump of wet toilet paper.

Seriously, I was going to puke, which would only make this humiliating incident even more humiliating.

"Joey?"

"I'm fine." I flung the toilet paper off my hand.

"Guys, go get her a blanket."

Both of the guys left. It was like they couldn't get out of here soon enough.

And I couldn't blame them.

This was the stuff of nightmares.

"What happened?" I looked away, unable to make eye contact with Jackson.

Any attraction he might have had to me was now gone. I had no doubt about that. This moment would be forever ingrained in his mind. I would be Joey who needed a garden hosey.

"We don't know yet." He nodded toward a car in the distance. It was no longer moving—a police cruiser had blocked its path. My keen powers of observation told me that must be the vehicle that knocked the Porta-Potty over. "From what my officer saw, it appears someone jammed a stick on the accelerator and set the car loose, headed right toward you. It's a good thing it didn't run you over."

"A stick?" That just confirmed my initial thoughts. This wasn't an accident. Not by any stretch of the imagination.

"It could have been worse," Jackson said. "I'm glad you're okay."

The officers came back with a blanket and a gallon of water, both of which Jackson happened to have in his sedan.

"I'm going to rinse myself before I do anything else," I said.

"Do you need help?" Jackson asked.

"I've got this." I grabbed the water and slipped behind another row of Porta-Potties.

When I did, I threw up.

———

I pulled the blanket closer around me as I sat beside Jackson in the car. I made sure none of my dirty parts touched his car. I had no doubt he'd probably have it detailed after this though.

I'd managed to get a lot of the waste products off me, but I was going to have to take a massive number of showers before I felt clean again. Maybe even use a Brillo pad on my skin. I wasn't sure.

For once in my life, I really didn't have anything to say. Seriously. This was so humiliating that I wanted to crawl under a rock.

"No one else could have this happen and still look as gorgeous as you," Jackson said.

"You're just being kind. I'm covered in poop and urine and toilet paper. There's nothing gorgeous about that."

He smiled, but it quickly slipped away. "You're always gorgeous, Joey."

Something about his words sounded sincere.

And if he was being sincere in a situation like this, then

. . . well, he was very convincing. I didn't even know what to say.

Thankfully, we pulled up to my house.

Also, thankfully, Zane didn't appear to be home.

"I'll wait down here while you get cleaned up," Jackson said.

I'd never taken a shower that felt so good. Never, ever. When I was done, I slipped on my favorite jean shorts and a T-shirt. I could finally hobble down the stairs without any help.

I knew I had to face Jackson, but I didn't want to. He stood from the couch when he heard me coming down the stairs, and he walked to the landing to wait for me.

Was that a twinkle of amusement in his otherwise serious eyes?

I took a step toward him, all my feistiness rising up. "You think this is funny?"

He raised his hands. "I didn't say that."

"All the guys at the station are going to be talking about this, aren't they?"

He finally nodded. "Probably."

"Do I still smell like I work for the sanitation department?"

He stepped closer—close enough for my nerves to sizzle.

"Nope." His face dipped toward me—toward my hair. My neck. Toward my delicate skin that now tingled with anticipation. "You smell like that new perfume."

"That's good. Because I used scalding-hot water and an entire bottle of body wash."

He chuckled and wrapped his arms around my neck in a friendly hug. But I melted into his embrace. I so needed a hug right now. I needed to know that Jackson wasn't totally repulsed by me . . . as most people would be.

He stepped away, and we were face to face. Close enough to kiss. Close enough that our gazes felt interlocked and unable to break.

Why did I always find myself in these situations with Jackson?

I knew. It was because there was something about the two of us that felt like a magnet and a metallic firecracker. We were drawn together—not that it meant we were meant to be together. Chemistry and attraction didn't assure a healthy relationship.

I stepped back. Why, oh why, couldn't I just do whatever I felt like doing whenever I felt like doing it? Especially when it came to dating. I wanted to jump in with both feet. I wanted to drown my sorrows in a man. I wanted romance to be my drug of choice—a drug that helped me forget all that was wrong in my life right now.

"We got a report back on that car," he said, helping me to the couch.

"Oh yeah? What happened to it?" I lowered myself on the cushions there, and Jackson sat beside me.

"Someone left their car running and ran up to an ATM machine at the shop beside the festival park. The next thing she knew, she saw her car barreling toward the Porta-Potties."

"How did that happen? You said something about a stick."

He nodded. "That's right. Apparently, someone saw an opportunity. They jammed a stake—probably one that a surveyor put in the ground—between the seat and the accelerator."

How fortuitous for them. "Any security footage?"

"My guys are checking on it now, but I doubt it. That shopping center is pretty old and the car was pretty far away. But if there's footage, we'll find it."

"One more crisis averted."

He frowned. "Joey, I'm really not sure you should go on with the show tomorrow night."

"Why wouldn't I?"

"Because someone hasn't been deterred yet. And the show would be the perfect place to make a statement."

_____

CHAPTER THIRTY-ONE

"HOW ABOUT WE go get some dinner?" Jackson asked a few minutes later.

We were still sitting on the couch, and I was still trying to process everything. It was going to take a while.

Jackson had mentioned dinner, but there was one problem with that. "I can't show my face in public ever again."

He squinted at me. "Then how are you going to do the meet and greet tomorrow?"

"I'll pretend to be someone else and block it out." Another thought hit. "You don't think any reporters were there and saw that whole Porta-Potty incident, do you?"

"I don't think so."

"But they're sneaky. They could have been there." Cameras seemed to be everywhere—except at crime scenes.

"Come on." He stood and offered his hand. "Let's eat. And then I have a few more leads to follow. I don't suppose you're interested in that, are you?"

"Leads? I love leads. To quote Raven Remington: 'leads are to a detective what water is to man.'"

"True." He took my arm. "But you look like you need a bite to eat first."

"Can we go to Fatty Shack?"

"Wherever you want."

I raised a finger and used my best teacher voice to warn, "And you can never speak a word about the Porta-Potty incident to anyone. Deal?"

He grinned. "Deal. Except when I write my police report."

We got to the restaurant, and I ordered crab cakes. Yes, I was supposed to be doing this raw-food thing so I could stay in shape. But sometimes nothing could replace fresh crabmeat that had been fried into a perfect patty and topped with tarter sauce and coleslaw and pressed between a buttered hot bun.

Fatty Shack was a local place located on the causeway between Roanoke Island and Nags Head. The place looked dated, and its décor was mostly old crab pots and buoys. But it had character, from its autographed photos of celebrities like Sandra Bullock and Tiger Woods to the strange scent of grease and disinfectant that constantly lingered in the air.

As we waited for our food, I grabbed my phone. Just out of curiosity, I searched for any video footage of the children's festival in Manteo. It seemed like something I should have done earlier, but I wanted to verify Helena's alibi. It should be pretty easy to do. In fact, the police had probably already done it.

"What are you looking at?" Jackson asked.

"One second." Sure enough, I found several videos of the family. But the one I wanted to see was front and center on my Internet search. The Briggs family had indeed performed the day of the accident. In fact, they were performing during the two hours between our rehearsal and the premiere.

I watched the video. Her family had dressed up like munchkins. They were each on their bellies, using their arms as legs, and wearing outfits that sold the look. They danced and flipped and reenacted children's stories.

It was entertaining. They had several other videos of their acts, which ranged from acrobatics to magic to juggling.

For part of the performance, they wore masks. Other times, they had special makeup on.

I let out a sigh. "Helena couldn't be behind this."

"We already checked out her alibi."

"I guess I wanted to see for myself." I leaned back and tried to think. As I sat there, I saw a girl walk past. She wore blue eyeshadow up to her brows.

I'd had no idea Dizzy would set such a trend.

Of all the things that I would help influence, I'd never thought makeup would be one of them.

"Should I go talk to her?" Jackson nodded toward the girl.

I glanced up at her again and saw her back to me but her cell phone out. "No, she's just taking a stealthie."

"A what?"

"It's when you take a selfie with someone intentionally in the background. Happens all the time."

"Good to know."

The waitress delivered our food, Jackson prayed over the meal, and then we dug in—to both our food and the investigation.

"So, if not Helena, who else does that leave us with?" I asked. "Gerrard has been unreachable."

"And what would his motive have been?" Jackson took a bite of his fish and chips.

"Carli said she thought she saw him sneaking away."

"There's no denying that he's a possibility."

"Then there's the security guard," I continued.

"But as you also noted, he has a limp from an old auto accident," Jackson said. "I confirmed it with two people—he's not faking. I doubt he could have scaled the scaffolding to sabotage things."

"Tim?" I hated to say his name.

Jackson studied me. "What do you think?"

I let out a sigh. "I really think Tim loves Carli. He seems devastated. The idea that he would go so far as to cut her harness so she would get out of the business and they can settle down and have kids? It seems over the top."

"I agree. Although, I've seen crimes committed for stranger reasons. But the main reason I don't think we should focus on him is because Carli hasn't been the only target. Most of these incidents have been directed at you."

"True."

Something at the edge of my consciousness was begging me for attention. After I took another bite of my crab cake sandwich, I pulled out my phone again and did a quick online search.

"What are you doing now?" Jackson asked, that familiar weary but amused look in his eyes.

"I want to watch the videos of the movie premiere."

"We've been through them."

"I know, but people keep posting them online—even though video cameras weren't supposed to be allowed." I hit one.

Jackson leaned closer to watch the video with me.

There was nothing new on this one. So I clicked another and then another.

It wasn't until the sixth video—right as I was about to give up—that something caught my eye.

"Look at this, Jackson." I pointed to the one I was talking about.

I paused it at just the right spot. If you looked closely in the rafters, there was a shadow.

"Do you see it?" I asked, my pulse spiking.

He took the phone from me and squinted. "There does appear to be someone in the scaffolding. Why didn't we see this in the videos we watched?"

"Notice the angle of this person. And the time—an hour before. This . . ." I glanced at her name at the bottom of the screen. "Cindy Lorro just posted this a few hours ago. Jackson, this shadow could be the person who did this."

This was great. We had a lead!

"But, Joey, we can't tell who this is." Jackson frowned as he studied the video. "It's too grainy."

"But this proves there was someone up there."

"We already know there was someone," Jackson reminded me. "The only way someone could have done this was to climb the scaffolding. What we need to know is who."

I wasn't going to let him discourage me. "But we also have a time frame now."

He nodded slowly and uncertainly. "That is true."

"And if you look at the video, you can clearly see Matt Myers is still on the side of the stage—although, he is talking to someone. Rutherford and the mayor are standing at the front. We can rule them out."

This time when he looked at me, there was a new look

in his eyes. Was that admiration? "You're getting better at this detective thing."

His compliment secretly made me glow. But I didn't let him know that. Instead, I pushed ahead. "I don't see Gerrard in this video."

"Our guys are actively looking for him. At this point, he's probably our best lead."

"Well, maybe your guys will find him and we'll get some answers. We can only hope."

Jackson leaned back and let out a long breath. He pushed the rest of his food away, and his face looked unusually melancholy.

"What's wrong?" I asked.

His concerned gaze met mine. "You do realize that this guy might try to strike again at the premiere, right?"

I nodded. "I do. But I also know there will be security precautions in place. I can't put my life on hold every time I'm in danger. Lately, that would mean I'd be in a permanent holding pattern."

"Yes, it would. But I'm not sure if I like this."

As the impact of his words hit me, I frowned. "Me either."

———

As soon as we walked outside and toward Jackson's vehicle, someone across the parking lot caught my eye. I grabbed Jackson's hand and pointed in the darkness.

"That person wearing a mask with my face on it keeps showing up," I said. I hated the way my voice crackled with a touch of fear. But it did.

"Let's find out who he or she is." Jackson took off toward the person.

As he did, the person turned around and tried to dart away.

But Jackson was faster. He caught the person, and they both toppled to the ground.

I held my breath as I waited to see what would play out next. Slowly—but driven by curiosity—I gravitated toward them.

Jackson pulled the mask off and . . . Abe sat there.

Zane's friend Abe.

His eyes met mine, and I expected to see apology or embarrassment. Instead, he looked excited.

My stomach churned with unease. What was going on here? Something felt wrong . . . and off.

"You want to explain yourself?" Jackson asked.

"There's nothing illegal about wearing a mask."

"You've been following Joey," Jackson said.

"We've just happened to be in the same place at the same time."

"You know I don't buy that. Now speak up before I take you down to the station."

Abe raised his hands. "Okay, okay. Calm down. Can I at least stand up?"

"Slowly and carefully," Jackson said.

Abe stood, his hands still in the air and that strangely amused look on his face. "What do you want to know?"

"I want to know what you're doing," Jackson said. There was definitely an edge to his voice, one that could strike fear in the most hardened of criminals.

Abe glanced at me—more like leered. "What can I say? I'm a big fan. Sorry I didn't admit that when we met."

"You two have met?" Jackson asked.

"He's a friend of Zane's—and Gerrard's."

"Do you always try to terrorize people you're a fan of?" Jackson asked.

"I wasn't trying to terrorize her," he said. "I was just trying to get her attention."

"Why would you want her attention?" Jackson asked his questions at a rapid-fire, no-nonsense pace.

"Who wouldn't want her attention? She's famous. She's beautiful. She's nice."

"And you thought that mask would . . ." My voice trailed off. I really had no idea what he was going for here. That I'd think he was a freak?

"I thought the mask would make you notice me."

"But all I noticed was the mask," I said.

"I figured I'd take whatever I could get."

"You were at the premiere," I muttered. That was the first time I remembered seeing that mask. Could Abe be the real culprit here?

"I was. And I know what you're thinking. I didn't sabotage the set."

"Do you know who did? Your friend Gerrard maybe?" I continued, sending a silent apology to Jackson for taking over his interrogation.

"I have no idea. Just because I'm your fan doesn't mean I did anything wrong."

But I wasn't so sure about that. Zane had said the man liked to compete in Spartan-like races and events. That meant he would be physically agile enough to do something like this. And with Gerrard being backstage, he could have gotten access.

It looked like I had a new suspect.

CHAPTER THIRTY-TWO

JACKSON DIDN'T HAVE ENOUGH to hold Abe, so he had to let him go. He assured me that the police were going to look into Abe further.

Nearly as soon as Jackson and I arrived at my place, Zane showed up. Things still felt awkward between us, but when he asked me if we could talk, I wondered exactly what was going on. I sensed this was serious.

I stepped outside, and the two of us walked around the house until we reached a deck overlooking the ocean. I sat in an Adirondack chair there and waited for him to begin.

"I'm going to Florida," he started, leaning with his elbows against the wooden railing overlooking the waves.

"Is it your dad? Is he okay?" His father had suffered some heart problems recently.

Zane raked a hand through his curls. "Dad seems to be doing fine. Truth is, I just need to get away."

"What's going on, Zane?"

He pulled his eyes to meet mine—but only for a moment. "You know I had drug problems when I was younger, right, Joey?"

My lungs felt like they might freeze as I anticipated what he might say. "I did know that. Yes."

"Right now I feel like there's too much temptation." His voice sounded even raspier than usual—raspy with emotion this time.

Whatever he was about to say, it wasn't easy for him. "What do you mean, Zane? How is there too much temptation?"

"I mean, it's the time of year that my friends are coming back into town. The friends who haven't always been a good influence. Who think recreational drugs are okay on occasion. I just can't be around them, Joey."

I licked my lips, trying to choose my words carefully and compassionately. "Have you been doing drugs again, Zane?"

He shook his head, but his gaze looked tortured and heavy. "No, but I almost did. Abe and a couple of other guys came over the other night—the night you asked me about. We were just chilling together, when they decided to unwind a little more than I thought necessary."

"Did you take my pain killers, Zane?" I didn't want to ask the question, but I had to know.

His jaw flexed, and he continued to look straight ahead. "Joey, I had no idea what happened to those drugs. I had no idea they were in my bag for that matter. I just found out that Abe stole them that day when you were at my friend's house. After he took a few, he slipped the bottle into the pocket of my sweatshirt. I didn't even know they were there. They must have fallen out when I packed that sweatshirt, and that's when you saw them."

"I see." I felt like he was telling the truth. He seemed truly sorry. But I really didn't like what was playing out here. Despite that, at least Zane had come to me.

He glanced at me and studied my expression. "I know you probably think less of me now."

Did I? I wasn't sure. But I did know it took a big person to come to me with this information instead of sweeping it under the rug. "The fact that you see this is a problem and that you're taking action says a lot. I'm not going to lie though. I'm disappointed this happened."

"So am I, Joey. I don't know what else to say."

"I'm going to have to report Abe to Jackson."

"I figured as much," Zane said.

A few minutes of silence slipped between us until I finally asked, "How long will you be gone?"

Zane shrugged, appearing like he had the weight of the world on his shoulders. "I'm not sure. Maybe a month or so. Enough for me to get a grip. I don't want to fall back into old habits again. That was a very dark time in my life, and I don't want to go back."

"I understand, and I'm glad you can see that. When are you leaving?"

"Tonight. I'm going to drive there. I figure the sooner I leave, the better." His gaze locked on mine. "Are you going to be okay? I know there's some crazy stuff going on."

"I'll be okay. You take care of yourself."

"Thanks, Joey."

———

Jackson had stayed at my place again, but we'd avoided any awkward, almost kissing moments. That was good. Honestly, my personal life—and my personal problems—had nearly made me so busy that I hadn't had as much time to dig into the mystery as I wanted.

There was a lot on the line here, and I needed to stay focused.

Just as I pulled my eyes open the next morning, I heard commotion downstairs. I was able to put my weight on my foot, so I got out of bed and quickly dressed. I wanted to brush my teeth first, but I figured I didn't have the time.

I'd also halfway expected Jackson to come get me, but he didn't. So I did the whole sliding-down-my-stairs-on-my-butt thing. Having a sprained ankle was so humbling. I'd managed to limp down yesterday but figured sliding might be easier. I was right.

When I reached the bottom, I glanced around. Where was Jackson?

A bad feeling churned in my gut. This couldn't be good.

That was definitely a commotion I'd heard downstairs.

I grabbed my crutches, determined to search the rest of the house. I hoped—and prayed—he was okay. I couldn't take anymore causalities in my life.

As soon as I rounded the staircase, I spotted Jackson. He was at the front door, bent down, with his phone shoved under his ear.

"Jackson?" I asked, creeping forward.

He turned toward me. As he did, I was able to catch a glance at what was on the other side of the doorway.

A body.

"It's okay, Joey," Jackson said.

"Who . . ." Was it Zane? That was all I could think about.

I peered over his shoulder.

I sucked in a breath at what I saw.

Rutherford lay there on his side, like he'd been dumped. What I wasn't sure about was whether he was dead or alive.

CHAPTER THIRTY-THREE

RUTHERFORD'S EYES FLUTTERED OPEN, and my heart rate slowed considerably. He was alive. Alive!

Jackson helped get him inside and to the couch, even though Rutherford appeared dazed and very confused.

Despite my state, I managed to fix Rutherford some coffee. Jackson carried it to him.

Detective Gardner had also shown up.

Jackson had called the paramedics, but Rutherford kept insisting he didn't need them.

I'd never seen Rutherford like this. He looked . . . well, pretty much like a normal guy who was down on his luck. It almost made me miss the haughty, arrogant Rutherford.

"So what happened, Rutherford?" Jackson asked.

Rutherford leaned back on my couch, looking dazed. "I'm still trying to figure it out. I remember walking to my beach house. Someone appeared out of nowhere. They tased me, and I must have passed out."

"Where did they take you?" Detective Gardner asked.

"That's the strange thing. I'm not sure." He rubbed his neck. "I mean, I woke up a few times, but everything is so hazy. I was bound and gagged. There was even a bag of some sort placed over my face. I couldn't see anything."

Jackson leaned toward him. "Do you remember anything? Anything at all?"

"I heard more than one voice."

My pulse spiked. That was good to know. There were at least two people in on this.

"The voice . . . it was a man's."

Also good to know.

"Did you recognize the voice?" Gardner asked.

"No, I didn't." Rutherford remained frozen a moment before shaking his head in obvious frustration. "I wish I could be more help."

"How about where you were kept?" Jackson continued. "Do you remember anything?"

He rubbed his neck again. "It was small. The walls felt like they were . . . wooden, I believe. That's what it seemed like when my hands brushed them. And the floor was cement."

Jackson's gaze remained intense and focused. "Was there AC?"

"It was hot. I feel like the space was some kind of outdoor area."

"That's a good start. Did you hear anything?" Jackson continued. "Even if it seems small and insignificant, it could still help."

"I thought I heard some cars going past, like we could be close to a street. I'm sorry. I wish I could help more." He swung his head back and forth. "But all I remember is praying desperately that I would live."

———

An hour later, Rutherford went to the hospital to get checked out, just as a precaution. Gardner had taken him, and the mayor was apparently going to meet him there.

That had left Jackson and me with nothing but time.

"Where do you think Rutherford was held?"

"I'm guessing it was one of those outdoor areas at a beach house."

I knew exactly what he was talking about. Most of the houses here were up on pilings. Many had areas underneath for storage or outdoor showers or changing areas. Someone could have cleared out one of those storage areas—which would most likely be framed in wood and set up on the driveway—and used that as a holding cell. If Rutherford had been bound and gagged, then no one would have heard him.

Jackson stood. I'd seen his wheels turning. I could see the fire in his eye to figure this out, and I knew something new had been ignited in him.

"I need to go talk to someone," he announced. "Matt Myers. I want to find out who he was talking to that night before the movie premiere started."

That was a great idea. "Can I go?"

"You really want to go?"

I nodded. "I do. I know I'm a lot of trouble and that I can hardly walk. But I want to go. I want answers."

Finally, he conceded with a quick nod. "Fine. But just promise me you'll stay out of it. Let me do the talking."

"Always."

He gave me a look. We both knew that wasn't true.

Despite that, we were in his sedan a few minutes later and headed down the road. I guessed he knew where Matt Myers lived. We finally pulled up to a brick ranch in a residential area of Manteo, a neighboring town.

One thing was for sure: there was no wooden storage

area beneath the house. Rutherford definitely hadn't been kept here.

When the bitter security guard answered the door, he looked none too happy to see me.

"You again." He started to slam the door, but Jackson stopped him.

"I'm here on police business."

His stance loosened when he saw Jackson's badge. "A working man. I can appreciate that."

I wanted to argue that I did work, but I knew that my work was child's play compared to so many. I couldn't even argue. I also knew I was blessed to have a fun career and get paid way more than I should for it.

Jackson showed him a still shot from the video. "Who were you talking to before the movie premiere?"

Matt's face reddened. "No one important."

"Why do you look uncomfortable then?"

"Because that man kept talking and talking to me," he said.

"What was he saying?"

"He wanted to know if he'd be able to meet Joey. If I'd met Joey. Could he get a backstage pass. He was very pushy and annoying."

"And he made it hard to do your job, didn't he?" Jackson asked. The subtext was clear: this man had served to distract Matt from the task at hand, and that may have led to this crime being committed.

He cringed. "He did."

"Why didn't you mention this when we questioned you?"

"It didn't seem important. If he'd gotten backstage, then yes, it would have obviously been important. Otherwise, he was just a crazy fan."

"What did he look like?"

He let out a sigh, as if he was annoyed at us. "He was a big guy. Dark hair. Seemed pretty fit."

"Could you go down to the station and meet with our sketch artist?"

He shrugged. "I suppose."

"If you could do that today, it would be great."

"I'll see what I can do then. Not for Ms. Hollywood over here, but for the sake of justice."

CHAPTER THIRTY-FOUR

JACKSON and I had to go to the festival area to check everything out. The premiere would start in three hours, and there were extra security precautions in place. This time there were more police officers. More random bags checked. And bomb-sniffing dogs were on the scene.

I was surprised when I walked behind the stage and saw Gerrard there messing with some wires.

Apparently, Jackson was surprised also.

Jackson strode up to him in law-enforcement mode. "We've been trying to reach you."

Gerrard froze from coiling some type of cord into a pile. He slowly rose to his feet. "I saw I'd missed some calls. I was on a camping trip. Primitive. No phones—or bathrooms, for that matter."

"You did this in the middle of a police investigation?" Jackson asked, looking mostly annoyed.

"No one ever told me not to go anywhere." He backed up, obviously on edge. His jaw muscle jumped, as if he was contemplating fight or flight.

"You can understand how this might make you look," Jackson continued.

I stayed situated behind Jackson, just in case things turned ugly. As my ankle often reminded me, I wouldn't be running away from anyone anytime soon.

"I didn't do anything," Gerrard barked. "You think I'd show back up here if I did?"

He had a point. He wouldn't be very wise if that was the case.

Jackson didn't seem as convinced. He still gave Gerrard a cold, hard stare. "Is there anything you'd like to tell us?"

"No, nothing." Gerrard shrugged, like the answer should be obvious.

"How about this: Someone said you were strangely absent in the hours between rehearsal and the premiere. Would you care to explain?"

"I was here!" He pressed his foot down as if to drive home his point.

"The whole time?"

He cringed. "My girlfriend did stop by. I went out to talk to her for a few minutes. But that was it. She didn't come backstage. You can check the log."

Jackson's jaw flexed this time. "Don't worry. I will. Will you be around after tonight?"

"If I need to be."

Jackson leveled his gaze with Gerrard. "You will."

———

Jackson had taken me home so I could change. Tonight would be a simplified version of our original plan. But at least people would get their money's worth and the children's wing would receive some additional funding.

And even though all the security precautions had been put in place, I still felt nervous. What if someone was still determined to ruin this?

I'd dressed more casually tonight, wearing my favorite jean shorts, a white tank top, and some sandals. My crutches were going to limit how much I could do.

There would be no stunts tonight. No, this was going to be a movie premiere. At the end, we'd have a meet and greet. Jackson would remain at my side.

I stood in the backstage area, trying to psych myself up for this, when someone called my name. I looked on the other side of the fence and saw Burly Reporter standing there.

After hesitating a moment, I walked toward him. "Yes?"

"Can we talk afterward?"

"Why would I do that?"

"I have something important to share with you," he said. "I was going to tell you sooner, but then I thought I'd let it be a surprise."

"You're scaring me."

"It's nothing bad. Not for you."

Okay, that freaked me out also. "I don't know what to say."

"Please, just trust me."

"I don't even know you."

"Look, at first I thought I needed a quote from you for something I was working on. Then I realized I didn't."

I had no idea what he was talking about. What was he working on? An article about my love life? "I don't know what to say."

"You won't want to miss this."

Said just like a serial killer trying to lure out his prey.

———

Sitting in my patched-up trailer—with no mysterious book bags this time—I ruminated a few more minutes on what I knew so far about the case.

Could Matt Myers be ruled out? Most likely.

Gerrard? Possibly.

Helena? She had a rock-solid alibi.

Tim? In my gut, I thought he'd told us the truth.

Then who else did that even leave?

I was floundering here. Raven Remington wouldn't be proud.

But it just seemed like every lead had dried up.

Someone was behind this

Was it one of the reporters? Abe? Another suspect we hadn't even discovered yet?

How about Jim, who owned the audio-visual company?

I'd joked about it being Rutherford or Eric. What if it was?

I doubted it. Rutherford hadn't staged his own abduction. And Eric was too prissy to take something this far. No, he'd just write tell-all books about it.

I squinted at the carpet and then picked up a sparkly piece of material. What was this?

Who knew what this trailer had been used for in the past? This piece of fabric didn't necessarily have to be connected with Carli's "accident." But I had found a similar piece of material on my hand that night when the fireworks had been thought to be gunfire.

An idea hit me.

I glanced at my watch. I didn't have much time. But this fabric could hold the answers.

I thought I'd seen a video that featured something similar.

I pulled up the footage I'd been looking for and held my breath.

Could this be it?

It wouldn't explain the whys of what had happened. But I had a feeling I knew who the bad guy was.

"Joey, you're on." Rutherford poked his head in the door, looking mostly like his old self. But I could see something different in his eyes—an unease.

I considered telling him my theory. But I didn't. Not yet.

If I was right, I didn't think this person had any more tricks to perform tonight. I could be desperately wrong though.

I went onstage and did my thing. I greeted people. Welcomed them. I tried to be as charming as possible.

But in the back of my mind, I couldn't stop thinking about what I'd discovered.

Finally, it was time for me to disappear backstage, and the movie would begin. I took my place, trying to steady my breathing. I needed to find Jackson and tell him what I'd learned. I saw him near the fence, talking to another officer.

When our eyes met, he came over to meet me. He squeezed my arm. "Good job out there."

"Jackson, I think I might know who's behind this—"

Before I could tell him who it was, the movie started. Only, it wasn't my movie.

It appeared to be some kind of documentary.

Jackson and I exchanged a look.

"Stay here," he whispered. "I want to finish this conversation."

Jackson stepped toward the gate, craning his neck so he could get a look at the screen. As soon as he did, someone appeared behind me.

With a gun. Shoved into my back.

"On the stage," the person muttered. "Now."

CHAPTER THIRTY-FIVE

I PUT my hands in the air as fear rippled through me. "Okay, okay. Just don't shoot."

"You need to go tell people the truth about what you do."

I recognized the voice. It was Helena. Cray-cray Helena. The one thing about crazy people was the fact that you never knew what would set them off. That meant I needed to proceed carefully.

"And what truth is that?" I finally asked, honestly having no clue what she was talking about.

"That you ruin relationships."

Okay, I seriously had no idea where this was going. "What in the world are you talking about?"

"You make all these movies with happy-ever-afters and set up people's expectations that they can get what you have, when they can't."

"That's not true. Movies can be escapes. They're supposed to be fun and make you think. They're not supposed to be ideals."

"Get onstage. Now!"

My knees trembled, but I did as she said. I carefully maneuvered my way toward the center.

"Joey!" Jackson called.

I glanced over at him, barely moving my head. He stood at the base of the stairs leading to the stage. He was crouched over, as if ready to pounce.

"I'm okay," I called.

"Helena, don't do this," Jackson said in all-out negotiator mode.

"It's too late. I'm doing this. And if you try to stop me, I'll shoot her."

The crowds had already started to murmur, wondering what was going on. They obviously knew this wasn't my movie. No, this was Helena's movie. The one entitled *I Hate You: A Realistic Look at Love.*

A woman was weeping on the screen, speaking to the camera all confessional-like.

The crowd's chatter became murmurs and gasps. I kept my steps steady, afraid one wrong move and Helena would accidentally pull the trigger.

"Everyone, this is Joey Darling," Helena said, spittle flying from her mouth. "She has something she'd like to tell you."

She shoved me toward the microphone. "Go ahead. Say it."

I glanced at her. "I don't know what you want me to say."

"Tell them the truth about relationships."

I glanced out at the crowd. Glanced to the side. Spotted Jackson and several other officers with their guns trained on us. Actually, trained on Helena. But, by default, on me.

I cleared my throat. "The truth is that relationships are hard," I started. "They're not what they're presented to be in the movies. Guys aren't always prince charmings, and women aren't always princesses. There are fights in real life. There's bad breath. There's moments you want to give up. There's no promise of happy-ever-after."

I had to keep talking, keenly aware of the gun shoved into my back.

"This is what real love looks like!" Helena shouted, pointing to another woman weeping on the screen. "It sucks."

"You don't have to do this, Helena," I whispered.

"Of course I do. Someone has to let Hollywood know that they're destroying America. Movies like *Family Secrets* make everyone think that some man is going to ride into your life and make things suddenly perfect."

"This wasn't a romance," I pointed out, knowing I needed to tread carefully.

"It's my mission in life to educate people," Helena said. "I'm taking the Lonely Girl's Last Stand."

Oh my . . .

"So you've been behind all this," I said. "You have one of your acts that uses some supposed magic. For that act, you have some sort of invisibility cloak. You call it your Harry Potter trick. It's really something you purchased that has metallic scales on it that reflects everything around it. It helps you to blend in wherever you go."

She gasped. "How did you know?"

"Because Raven Remington is my role model. What I'm not sure about is whether or not you were targeting Carli or me."

"I'm targeting Hollywood."

"I see."

"I thought those bottles that I stole from your ex's trash can might make you speak the truth about relationships," she continued. "I know what happened between you."

I tugged at my collar, not wanting to rehash that in front of an audience. "Is that right?"

"But no. You still didn't come forward with the truth. I was annoyed—that's why I left my brother's snake in the car."

She was unhinged. So unhinged. "And kidnapping my manager?"

"I thought he might have some pull. But instead he wept like a baby and annoyed the snot out of me. I couldn't keep him under my house anymore."

My heart went out to Rutherford. I knew that statement would humiliate him, especially when this went viral. And this would go viral. However it ended, this was a social media lover's dream.

Jackson stepped onstage. "Let her go, Helena."

"No, this needs to play out. This is the Lonely Girl's—"

"Last Stand," he finished. "I know. Men are jerks sometimes. But the beautiful part about marriage and relationships are when two broken people with all their faults and shortcomings decide to stick it out, despite the hard times."

"What's romantic about shortcomings?" Helena snorted.

"They're real," Jackson said. "There's something refreshing about realizing your love story doesn't have to be perfect to be great."

She was becoming more unhinged by the minute. I had to do something to at least get her away from me so Jackson would have a chance to take her down.

That was when I remembered my famous move. Baloney. Below-knee. Raven had used it, but I'd taught it to her because my dad had taught it to me.

It might be my only chance here.

If it didn't work, I had a captive audience that would get a real-life show playing out before their eyes.

"Ask anyone out here. Romance isn't perfect. Am I right?" Jackson asked the audience.

What was Jackson doing? I had to trust him.

"My husband and I have been married for forty years!" one woman yelled.

"My wife drives me crazy—but I love her!"

"Real love is better than any of that Hollywood stuff. Movies don't keep you warm at night and won't take care of you when you're old."

I could feel Helena moving behind me, but I couldn't see what she was doing. The gun didn't seem to be pressed into my back quite as hard.

I glanced at Jackson again out of the corner of my eye. He was creeping closer.

He gave me a subtle nod.

At once, I pulled my leg up and then rammed it back into Helena's knee. She let out a cry of pain.

When she did, I ducked to the ground and rolled—another move I'd learned from Raven.

Jackson swooped in and tackled Helena, taking her gun from her.

The crowd cheered.

Other officers rushed onto the stage.

Lonely Girl's Last Stand was over. Finally.

CHAPTER THIRTY-SIX

AFTER A SMALL BREAK, I announced to everyone who came that the show must go on. That stories were meant to be an escape, meant to be entertainment, and I could tell that everyone needed a little distraction from real life right now.

So the show did go on.

Family Secrets played on the screen, and the audience was captive—other than a few reporters who had gathered at the gate, trying to talk to me about what had just happened. I ignored them, not ready to answer any questions. Not yet. I was still shaken.

The police had already debriefed me. Detective Gardner had taken Helena to the station for further questioning. Apparently, from what I'd overheard, one of Helena's brothers had been helping her. He was the one who'd distracted Matt Myers while Helena had snuck backstage to damage the harness.

Because of a special suit she used for her acts, she was able to sneak over the fence and backstage. She'd even gotten into the trailer to plant the bomb. I'd also heard her say she'd learned how to make a bomb online.

I escaped to the trailer to compose myself. Five minutes later, Jackson came inside and sat beside me on the stiff tweed couch.

"Are you okay?" His hand rested on my knee.

I nodded uncertainly. "I am. I think. Thank you."

"You used some pretty smart moves out there. You actually are much better than I thought you'd be at keeping a cool head in a hot situation."

"Thank you." I was pretty sure that was the right response. Then I began replaying what had happened. "I can't believe Helena did all this because she was bitter about happy endings."

"Some people take love and romance very seriously."

I shifted. "Speaking of which, we never did talk about that kiss."

My throat clenched. But what better time to talk about this than now? I'd been avoiding it for so long, coming up with excuse after excuse.

Jackson turned to face me more. "I know."

"Jackson, I—"

"You want to talk about that kiss, don't you?" A smeyes crossed his face again.

"You knew that?"

He nodded. "Yeah, I knew that. I figured we had other stuff we should probably focus on."

"Probably."

He released a breath and scooted closer. My heart pounded furiously in my ears, especially when his hands went to my arms. When his eyes stared at my lips. When my body felt as lit up as a Christmas tree.

"I was prepared to try and convince you that you were ready for a relationship."

I swallowed hard. "You were?"

He grimaced. "And then this week happened."

I released my pent-up energy in a whoosh of air from my lungs. What did that mean? Did I want to know?

I could hardly breathe as I waited for him to continue. I had no idea where he was going with this. Would it be the same route as a happy-ending movie? Or would it be a tragedy?

"Relationships are difficult. We all bring baggage into them. But I can see that Eric still affects you, Joey."

Great, we weren't even dating, and he was already breaking up with me. "I don't love him anymore, Jackson."

"I didn't say you love him. But I think you have things unresolved from your relationship. Things that may not seem like a big deal now—or maybe they do—but I don't think you're ready to jump into another relationship. Not a real one."

As the truth of his words hit me, I glanced at my tangled fingers in my lap. "It's easy to jump into one that will help me forget. That's what I've always done."

Jackson's warm gaze met mine. "You and me . . . I want it to be different. I want to start on solid ground. You know what I mean?"

I nodded, even though I could hardly breathe.

He gently rubbed his thumb against my jaw, his gaze mesmerizing me.

"So I don't know what you were going to tell me about that kiss," he murmured. "But maybe we could save that conversation until you have some resolution."

His words caused such a reaction in me that I threw my arms around him and held him close.

He got me. He actually got me.

He let out a soft chuckle. "What's this for?"

"For being more of a man than anyone I've ever met. Except my dad."

His embrace tightened. "You deserve someone who treats you like a lady, Joey."

I kept hugging him. I didn't want to ever let go.

Just as I pulled away, someone knocked on the trailer door.

I could see the top of Burly Reporter's head.

"Do you want me to tell him to go away?" Jackson asked.

"No, I want to hear what he has to say. Will you stay?"

"Always."

CHAPTER THIRTY-SEVEN

BURLY REPORTER STEPPED into the trailer. "I hoped I might find you here."

"Why would you want to find me?" This was one more mystery I needed to wrap up.

"I wanted to show you this." He plopped the latest issue of *Persons* magazine down in front of me. "Before it hits the stands."

I sucked in a deep breath as I picked it up. My face was on the cover.

This could be very bad.

"I'm not sure I want to read this," I said.

"You'll want to."

I held my breath as I opened the cover and riffled through the pages until I found his article. "Eric Lauderdale: Captain Hotheaded Abuser" the headline read.

I glanced up at Burly Reporter man, and he nodded, as if urging me to continue.

Jackson read over my shoulder with me.

"'Miriam Rodriguez, who worked as a maid at Eric Lauderdale and Joey Darling's home while they were married, revealed in a startling interview that Lauderdale was abusive to Darling.'"

My heart thumped so hard in my ears that I could hardly hear anything else.

I couldn't stop reading.

Miriam had done an interview? I couldn't believe it. She'd been so quiet and timid.

The forty-something woman had lived in our house with us for a good three years, and I'd always liked her. I'd been surprised when she never came to the hospital to see me after the accident. This was explaining why.

"'He was always awful to her,' Miriam said. 'Screaming at her. Putting her down. Delighting in her failures. Demeaning her successes.'"

My heart pounded even harder.

"'But I came home one day and saw Ms. Darling at the bottom of the stairs. Her head was bloody, and Eric had just left. I saw his car pulling away. He'd left her there to die. To suffer. To whatever. That was when I knew he was a heartless excuse for a man.'"

Miriam had seen that? Why hadn't she helped me? Why had she left me there?

Jackson's hand squeezed my waist more tightly, as if he recognized my inner turmoil.

"'I went to help her, but as I did, I realized Mr. Lauderdale had come back. He threatened to deport me if I told anyone. He gave me ten thousand dollars and told me to leave. So I did. It wasn't my proudest moment. Not by a long shot. But I was scared for myself and for my daughter. But now I want to make things right. I have to.'"

I glanced back up at Burly Reporter. "She talked to you?"

He nodded. "I heard Eric had a temper and a mean

streak—a different image than he presented to the media. So I started digging. I read all the trash he was talking about you, and it raised red flags in my head. So I started digging harder."

"Does . . . does Eric know about this?" The words hardly left my throat.

"I came to him for a comment, but he declined. But he was as mad as a hornet. Said he'd sue me if I published any of my absurd theories."

"When does this go live?" I asked.

"Tomorrow. I just wanted you to know first. This needed to be told, and I'm sorry that I didn't include you in it. My mom was in a bad relationship, and I didn't want to risk you being raked through the mud. But if you ever want to tell your story . . ."

"I'll keep you in mind."

Maybe Eric would finally get what was coming to him. It wasn't necessarily the way I would have planned it, but things were happening that were just going to happen. I had no power to stop them, and I wasn't sure I would even if I could.

I hoped my ex would learn his lesson, once and for all.

And before anyone else got hurt.

———

The next day, I picked up my suitcase, feeling a strange mix of apprehension and excitement.

I carried it to the door, ready for another adventure. This one was a personal one, a catharsis of sorts.

Jackson arrived just on time. He didn't know what exactly was going on, but he was giving me a ride to the airport anyway.

It wasn't until we were in his truck and heading down the road that he finally spoke.

"You want to tell me what's going on? Are you going back to LA?"

"No!" Of course he might think that. "I'm sorry you thought that. But no, I'll be back in a couple of days."

"Do you want to share where you're going?"

I dragged my gaze from out the window and glanced at him. "I'm skipping a day."

"What are you talking about?"

I released a heavy breath. "Tomorrow would have been my wedding anniversary. It would have been three years. And I don't want to remember that day because it was a huge mistake."

"So how to you plan on skipping a day?"

"It's slightly complicated. But I'm leaving today, and I'll be traveling through Europe for thirty hours. When I get to Australia, it will be Friday."

"You haven't officially skipped—"

I raised a finger to stop him. "Let me have my moment."

He paused and nodded. "I will."

"No, I know it's impossible to actually skip a day. But I'll be in the air, going from time zone to time zone. I'll be sleeping for most of that. And it will be like our anniversary never happened."

"It's unconventional, but I like it. I think you can safely say that Eric won't be getting many jobs."

"Hollywood rewards bad behavior, Jackson."

"Maybe if he was a good actor . . ."

That made me smile.

Jackson reached over and squeezed my hand. "I look forward to seeing you when you get back, Joey. You are coming back, right?"

I smiled. "Yeah, I am. I have to find my dad still." I held up a piece of paper. "My super-stalker fan club came through. I found this outside of my house this morning."

"What does it say?"

I cleared my throat. "Good job, Joey. Now you're catching on. As promised, here's a clue. Your father is closer than he seems."

Jackson glanced at me. "What does that mean?"

I shook my head. "I have no idea."

"I guess you'll find out."

"I will?"

"You always do, Joey. The same persistence that's gotten you far in Hollywood will get you far in this case. I'm sure. And I'll be there for you when you need me."

"You will?"

The smeyes returned. "Of course I will."

COMING NEXT: BLOOPER FREAK

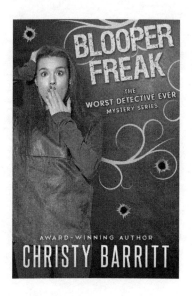

Joey's friend is accused of murder and the mysterious fan club stalking Joey has answers she desperately needs. With each new case, the Hollywood starlet edges closer to the truth about her missing father.

Get your copy at Amazon.

ALSO BY CHRISTY BARRITT:

THE WORST DETECTIVE EVER:

Ready to Fumble (**Book 1**)

I'm not really a private detective. I just play one on TV. Joey Darling, better known to the world as Raven Remington, detective extraordinaire, is trying to separate herself from her invincible alter ego. She played the spunky character for five years on the hit TV show *Relentless*, which catapulted her to fame and into the role of Hollywood's sweetheart. When her marriage falls apart, her finances dwindle to nothing, and her father disappears, Joey finds herself on the Outer Banks of North Carolina, trying to piece her life back together away from the limelight. A woman finds Raven—er, Joey—and insists on hiring her fictional counterpart to find a missing boyfriend. When someone begins staging crime scenes to match an episode of Relentless, Joey has no choice but to get involved.

Reign of Error (**Book 2**)

Sometimes in life, you just want to yell "Take two!" When a Polar Plunge goes terribly wrong and someone dies in the icy water, former TV detective Joey Darling wants nothing to do with the subsequent investigation. But when her picture is found in the dead man's wallet and witnesses place her as the last person seen speaking with the man, she realizes she's been cast in a role she never wanted: suspect. Joey makes the dramatic mistake of challenging the killer on camera, and now it's a race to find the bad guy before he finds her. Danger abounds and suspects are harder to find than the Lost Colony of Roanoke Island. Will Joey find the killer? Or will her mistake-riddled streak continue?

Safety in Blunders (**Book 3**)

My name is Joey Darling, and I'm a disgrace to imaginary detectives everywhere. When actress Joey Darling discovers a mermaid tail with drops of fresh blood on it while hiking in a remote nature preserve, she knows something suspicious is going on. As details surface, Joey realizes she's dealing with a problem she has encountered one too many times: someone desperate for fame who falls victim to a predator. With the help of her neighbor Zane Oakley and the opposition of local detective Jackson Sullivan, Joey hunts for answers, unaware of the deadly net in which she's about to entangle herself. Joey knows she's a fish out of water when it comes to cracking cases, but can she use her talent—acting—to help find the missing woman? Or will Joey end up swimming with sharks?

Join the Flub (**Book 4**)

There's no business like show business . . . especially when a killer is involved. Joey Darling's local movie premiere was supposed to be a win-win for everyone involved. But things go awry when the event is sabotaged ,and Joey's stunt double is seriously injured. Police fear the intended target was actually Joey. Detective Jackson Sullivan and neighbor Zane Oakley—two men competing for Joey's affection—insist on trading off guard duty until the bad guy is behind bars. To make matters even worse, Joey's ex shows up right before the release of his tell-all book about his life with the Hollywood sweetheart. Someone seems determined to create real-life drama. But Joey isn't one to be deterred. Though a movie-worthy villain wants to pull the plug on this production—and maybe even on a few people's lives—Joey is determined that the show must go on.

Blooper Freak (**Book 5**)

Joey's friend is accused of murder and the mysterious fan club stalking Joey has answers she desperately needs. With each new case, the Hollywood starlet edges closer to the truth about her missing father.

Flaw Abiding Citizen (**Book 6**)

Coming in November

SQUEAKY CLEAN MYSTERIES:

Hazardous Duty (**Book 1**)

On her way to completing a degree in forensic science, Gabby St. Claire drops out of school and starts her own crime-scene cleaning business. When a routine cleaning job uncovers a murder weapon the police overlooked, she realizes that the wrong person is in jail. But the owner of the weapon is a powerful foe . . . and willing to do anything to keep Gabby quiet. With the help of her new neighbor, Riley Thomas, a man whose life and faith fascinate her, Gabby seeks to find the killer before another murder occurs.

Suspicious Minds (**Book 2**)

In this smart and suspenseful sequel to *Hazardous Duty*, crime-scene cleaner Gabby St. Claire finds herself stuck doing mold remediation to pay the bills. Her first day on the job, she uncovers a surprise in the crawlspace of a dilapidated home: Elvis, dead as a doornail and still wearing his blue-suede shoes. How could she possibly keep her nose out of a case like this?

It Came Upon a Midnight Crime (**Book 2.5, a Novella**)

Someone is intent on destroying the true meaning of Christmas—at least, destroying anything that hints of it. All around crime-scene cleaner Gabby St. Claire's hometown, anything pointing to Jesus as "the reason for the season" is being sabotaged. The crimes become more twisted as dismembered body parts are found at the vandalisms. Someone is determined to destroy Christmas . . . but Gabby is just as determined to find the Grinch and let peace on earth and goodwill prevail.

Organized Grime (**Book 3**)

Gabby St. Claire knows her best friend, Sierra, isn't guilty of killing three people in what appears to be an eco-terrorist attack. But Sierra has disappeared, her only contact a frantic phone call to Gabby proclaiming she's being hunted. Gabby is determined to prove her friend is innocent and to keep Sierra alive. While trying to track down the real perpetrator, Gabby notices a disturbing trend at the crime scenes she's cleaning, one that ties random crimes together —and points to Sierra as the guilty party. Just what has her friend gotten herself involved in?

Dirty Deeds (**Book 4**)

"Promise me one thing. No snooping. Just for one week." Gabby St. Claire knows that her fiancé's request is a simple one she should be able to honor. After all, Riley's law school reunion and attorneys' conference at a posh resort is a chance for them to get away from the mysteries Gabby often finds herself involved in as a crime-scene cleaner. Then an old friend of Riley's goes missing. Gabby suspects one of Riley's buddies might be behind the disappearance. When the missing woman's mom asks Gabby for help, how can she say no?

The Scum of All Fears (**Book 5**)

Gabby St. Claire is back to crime-scene cleaning and needs help after a weekend killing spree fills her work docket. A serial killer her fiancé put behind bars has escaped. His last words to Riley were: *I'll get out, and I'll get even.* Pictures of Gabby are found in the man's prison cell, messages are left for Gabby at crime scenes, someone keeps slipping in and out of her apartment, and her temporary assistant disappears. The search for answers becomes darker when Gabby realizes she's dealing with a criminal who is truly the scum of the earth. He will do anything to make Gabby's and Riley's lives a living nightmare.

To Love, Honor, and Perish (**Book 6**)

Just when Gabby St. Claire's life is on the right track, the unthinkable happens. Her fiancé, Riley Thomas, is shot and in life-threatening condition only a week before their wedding. Gabby is determined to figure out who pulled the trigger, even if investigating puts her own life at risk. As she digs deeper into the case, she discovers secrets better left alone. Doubts arise in her mind, and the one man with answers lies on death's doorstep. Then an old foe returns and tests everything Gabby is made of—physically, mentally, and spiritually. Will all she's worked for be destroyed?

Mucky Streak (**Book 7**)

Gabby St. Claire feels her life is smeared with the stain of tragedy. She takes a short-term gig as a private investigator—a cold case that's eluded detectives for ten years. The mass murder of a wealthy family seems impossible to solve, but Gabby brings more clues to light. Add to the mix a flirtatious client, travels to an exciting new city, and some quirky —albeit temporary—new sidekicks, and things get complicated. With every new development, Gabby prays that her "mucky streak" will end and the future will become clear. Yet every answer she uncovers leads her closer to danger— both for her life and for her heart.

Foul Play (**Book 8**)

Gabby St. Claire is crying "foul play" in every sense of the phrase. When the crime-scene cleaner agrees to go undercover at a local community theater, she discovers more than backstage bickering, atrocious acting, and rotten writing. The female lead is dead, and an old classmate who has staked everything on the musical production's success is about to go under. In her dual role of investigator and star of the show, Gabby finds the stakes rising faster than the opening-night curtain. She must face her past and make monumental decisions, not just about the play but also concerning her future relationships and career. Will Gabby find the killer before the curtain goes down—not only on the play, but also on life as she knows it?

Broom and Gloom (**Book 9**)

Gabby St. Claire is determined to get back in the saddle again. While in Oklahoma for a forensic conference, she meets her soon-to-be stepbrother, Trace Ryan, an up-and-coming country singer. A woman he was dating has disappeared, and he suspects a crazy fan may be behind it. Gabby agrees to investigate, as she tries to juggle her conference, navigate being alone in a new place, and locate a woman who may not want to be found. She discovers that sometimes taking life by the horns means staring danger in the face, no matter the consequences.

Dust and Obey (**Book 10**)

When Gabby St. Claire's ex-fiancé, Riley Thomas, asks for her help in investigating a possible murder at a couples retreat, she knows she should say no. She knows she should run far, far away from the danger of both being around Riley and the crime. But her nosy instincts and determination take precedence over her logic. Gabby and Riley must work together to find the killer. In the process, they have to confront demons from their past and deal with their present relationship.

Thrill Squeaker (**Book 11**)

An abandoned theme park. An unsolved murder. A decision that will change Gabby's life forever. Restoring an old amusement park and turning it into a destination resort seems like a fun idea for former crime-scene cleaner Gabby St. Claire. The side job gives her the chance to spend time with her friends, something she's missed since beginning a new career. The job turns out to be more than Gabby bargained for when she finds a dead body on her first day. Add to the mix legends of Bigfoot, creepy clowns, and ghostlike remnants of happier times at the park, and her stay begins to feel like a rollercoaster ride. Someone doesn't want the decrepit Mythical Falls to open again, but just how far is this person willing to go to ensure this venture fails? As the stakes rise and danger creeps closer, will Gabby be able to restore things in her own life that time has destroyed— including broken relationships? Or is her future closer to the fate of the doomed Mythical Falls?

Swept Away, a Honeymoon Novella (Book 11.5)

Finding the perfect place for a honeymoon, away from any potential danger or mystery, is challenging. But Gabby's longtime love and newly minted husband, Riley Thomas, has done it. He has found a location with a nonexistent crime rate, a mostly retired population, and plenty of opportunities for relaxation in the warm sun. Within minutes of the newlyweds' arrival, a convoy of vehicles pulls up to a nearby house, and their honeymoon oasis is destroyed like a sandcastle in a storm. Despite Gabby's and Riley's determination to keep to themselves, trouble comes knocking at their door—literally—when a neighbor is abducted from the beach directly outside their rental. Will Gabby and Riley be swept away with each other during their honeymoon . . . or will a tide of danger and mayhem pull them under?

Cunning Attractions (Book 12)

Politics. Love. Murder. Radio talk show host Bill

McCormick is in his prime. He's dating a supermodel, his book is a bestseller, and his ratings have skyrocketed during the heated election season. But when Bill's ex-wife, Emma Jean, turns up dead, the media and his detractors assume the opinionated loudmouth is guilty of her murder. Bill's on-air rants about his demon-possessed ex don't help his case. Did someone realize that Bill was the perfect scape-goat? Or could Bill have silenced his Ice Queen ex once and for all? As Gabby comes closer to casting her vote for the guilty party, the stakes rise, tensions heat, and her own life is endangered. Will she be able to do a recount as votes are cast about who the murderer is? Or was this whole crime rigged from the start?

Clean Getaway (Book 13)

Gabby St. Claire Thomas has been given the opportunity of a lifetime: heading up a privately funded Cold Case Squad and handpicking the team members. Persnickety Evie Manson and nerdy Sherman Gilbert join forces with Gabby to bring justice and solace to families still wanting answers. On their first case, the Squad discovers that the murders of Ron and Margie Simmons are more than cold—they're frozen solid. The couple's anniversary celebration ended as a double homicide, and ten years later their daughter is still waiting for answers. But who would want to kill the loving couple? What kind of secrets were hiding beneath their cheery, All American exteriors? With every new lead, someone tries to sabotage their investigation . . . but the team might just end up being their own worst enemies. As a deadline presses in, can Gabby and her Squad bring the heat? Or will this cold-case killer make a clean getaway?

While You Were Sweeping, a **Riley Thomas Novella**

Riley Thomas is trying to come to terms with life after a traumatic brain injury turned his world upside down. Away from everything familiar—including his crime-scene-cleaning former fiancée and his career as a social-rights attorney—he's determined to prove himself and regain his old life. But when he claims he witnessed his neighbor shoot and kill someone, everyone thinks he's crazy. When all evidence of the crime disappears, even Riley has to wonder if he's losing his mind.

Note: *While You Were Sweeping* is a spin-off mystery written in conjunction with the Squeaky Clean series featuring crime-scene cleaner Gabby St. Claire.

THE SIERRA FILES:

Pounced (Book 1)
Animal-rights activist Sierra Nakamura never expected to stumble upon the dead body of a coworker while filming a project nor get involved in the investigation. But when someone threatens to kill her cats unless she hands over the "information," she becomes more bristly than an angry feline. Making matters worse is the fact that her cats—and the investigation—are driving a wedge between her and her boyfriend, Chad. With every answer she uncovers, old hurts rise to the surface and test her beliefs. Saving her cats might mean ruining everything else in her life. In the fight for survival, one thing is certain: either pounce or be pounced.

Hunted (Book 2)
Who knew a stray dog could cause so much trouble? Newlywed animal-rights activist Sierra Nakamura Davis must face her worst nightmare: breaking the news she eloped with Chad to her ultra-opinionated tiger mom. Her perfectionist parents have planned a vow-renewal ceremony

at Sierra's lush childhood home, but a neighborhood dog ruins the rehearsal dinner when it shows up toting what appears to be a fresh human bone. While dealing with the dog, a nosy neighbor, and an old flame turning up at the wrong times, Sierra hunts for answers. Her journey of discovery leads to more than just who committed the crime.

Pranced (Book 2.5, a Christmas novella)

Sierra Nakamura Davis thinks spending Christmas with her husband's relatives will be a real Yuletide treat. But when the animal-rights activist learns his family has a reindeer farm, she begins to feel more like the Grinch. Even worse, when Sierra arrives, she discovers the reindeer are missing. Sierra fears the animals might be suffering a worse fate than being used for entertainment purposes. Can Sierra set aside her dogmatic opinions to help get the reindeer home in time for the holidays? Or will secrets tear the family apart and ruin Sierra's dream of the perfect Christmas?

Rattled (Book 3)

"What do you mean a thirteen-foot lavender albino ball python is missing?" Tough-as-nails Sierra Nakamura Davis isn't one to get flustered. But trying to balance being a wife and a new mom with her crusade to help animals is proving harder than she imagined. Add a missing python, a high maintenance intern, and a dead body to the mix, and Sierra becomes the definition of rattled. Can she balance it all—and solve a possible murder—without losing her mind?

Random Acts of Murder (**Book 1**)

When Holly Anna Paladin is given a year to live, she embraces her final days doing what she loves most—random acts of kindness. But one of her extreme good deeds goes horribly wrong, implicating her in a string of murders. Holly is suddenly thrust into a different kind of fight for her life. Could it also be random that the detective assigned to the case is her old high school crush and present-day nemesis? Will Holly find the killer before he ruins what is left of her life? Or will she spend her final days alone and behind bars?

Random Acts of Deceit (**Book 2**)

"Break up with Chase Dexter, or I'll kill him." Holly Anna Paladin never expected such a gut-wrenching ultimatum. With home invasions, hidden cameras, and bomb threats, Holly must make some serious choices. Whatever she decides, the consequences will either break her heart or break her soul. She tries to match wits with the Shadow

Man, but the more she fights, the deeper she's drawn into the perilous situation. With her sister's wedding problems and the riots in the city, Holly has nearly reached her breaking point. She must stop this mystery man before someone she loves dies. But the deceit is threatening to pull her under . . . six feet under.

Random Acts of Malice (**Book 3**)

When Holly Anna Paladin's boyfriend, police detective Chase Dexter, says he's leaving for two weeks and can't give any details, she wants to trust him. But when she discovers Chase may be involved in some unwise and dangerous pursuits, she's compelled to intervene. Holly gets a run for her money as she's swept into the world of horseracing. The stakes turn deadly when a dead body surfaces and suspicion is cast on Chase. At every turn, more trouble emerges, making Holly question what she holds true about her relationship and her future. Just when she thinks she's on the homestretch, a dark horse arises. Holly might lose everything in a nail-biting fight to the finish.

Random Acts of Scrooge (**Book 3.5**)

Christmas is supposed to be the most wonderful time of the year, but a real-life Scrooge is threatening to ruin the season's good will. Holly Anna Paladin can't wait to celebrate Christmas with family and friends. She loves everything about the season—celebrating the birth of Jesus, singing carols, and baking Christmas treats, just to name a few. But when a local family needs help, how can she say no? Holly's community has come together to help raise funds to save the home of Greg and Babette Sullivan, but a Bah-Humburgler has snatched the canisters of cash. Holly and her boyfriend, police detective Chase Dexter, team up to catch the Christmas crook. Will they succeed in collecting enough cash to cover the Sullivans' overdue bills? Or will someone succeed in ruining Christmas for all those involved?

Random Acts of Greed (Book 4)

Help me. Don't trust anyone. Do-gooder Holly Anna Paladin can't believe her eyes when a healthy baby boy is left on her doorstep. What seems like good fortune quickly turns into concern when blood spatter is found on the bottom of the baby carrier. Something tragic—maybe deadly —happened in connection with the infant. The note left only adds to the confusion. What does it mean by "Don't trust anyone"? Holly is determined to figure out the identity of the baby. Is his mom someone from the inner-city youth center where she volunteers? Or maybe the connection is through Holly's former job as a social worker? Even worse— what if the blood belongs to the baby's mom? Every answer Holly uncovers only leads to more questions. A sticky web of intrigue captures her imagination until she's sure of only one thing: she must protect the baby at all cost.

Random Acts of Fraud (Book 5)

Vintage-loving Holly Anna Paladin finds online dating uncouth and unbecoming. But, in an attempt to overcome her romantic slump, her BFF convinces Holly to give it a shot. When Holly is stood up on her first date, she's halfway relieved . . . until she discovers the reason isn't because her cyber matchup has cold feet. Instead she stumbles upon him in a classic Mustang, deader than good old-fashioned manners. Holly's had enough with investigating crime and leaves her ex-boyfriend, Detective Chase Dexter, to solve this mystery. But Holly is somehow connected to this murder, and someone is determined to keep her in the thick of things. She hopes it's not Drew Williams, the handsome funeral director who's trying to sweep her off her feet. Before more people are hurt, Holly is determined to unmask the pretender in her life. But can she keep her feelings for Chase locked away? Or will Holly end up losing her heart to him all over again? She must solve the case before someone pulls the plug on her profile . . . and deletes her permanently.

CAROLINA MOON SERIES:

Home Before Dark (**Book 1**)

Nothing good ever happens after dark. Country singer Daleigh McDermott's father often repeated those words. Now, her father is dead. As she's about to flee back to Nashville, she finds his hidden journal with hints that his death was no accident. Mechanic Ryan Shields is the only one who seems to believe Daleigh. Her father trusted the man, but her attraction to Ryan scares her. She knows her life and career are back in Nashville and her time in the sleepy North Carolina town is only temporary. As Daleigh and Ryan work to unravel the mystery, it becomes obvious that someone wants them dead. They must rely on each other—and on God—if they hope to make it home before the darkness swallows them.

Gone By Dark (**Book 2**)

Ten years ago, Charity White's best friend, Andrea, was abducted as they walked home from school. A decade later, when Charity receives a mysterious letter that promises answers, she returns to North Carolina in search of closure. With the help of her new neighbor, Police Officer Joshua Haven, Charity begins to track down mysterious clues concerning her friend's abduction. They soon discover that they must work together or both of them will be swallowed by the looming darkness.

Wait Until Dark (**Book 3**)

A woman grieving broken dreams. A man struggling to regain memories. A secret entrenched in folklore dating back two centuries. Antiquarian Felicity French has no clue the trouble she's inviting in when she rescues a man outside her grandma's old plantation house during a treacherous snowstorm. All she wants is to nurse her battered heart and wounded ego, as well as come to terms with her past. Now she's stuck inside with a stranger sporting an old bullet wound and forgotten hours. Coast Guardsman Brody Joyner can't remember why he was out in such perilous weather, how he injured his head, or how a strange key got into his pocket. He also has no idea why his pint-sized savior has such a huge chip on her shoulder. He has no choice but to make the best of things until the storm passes. Brody and Felicity's rocky start goes from tense to worse when danger closes in. Who else wants the mysterious key that somehow ended up in Brody's pocket? Why? The unlikely duo quickly becomes entrenched in an adventure of a lifetime, one that could have ties to local folklore and Felicity's ancestors. But sometimes the past leads to darkness . . . darkness that doesn't wait for anyone.

Light the Dark (**a Christmas novella**)

Nine months pregnant, Hope Solomon is on the run and fearing for her life. Desperate for warmth, food, and shelter, she finds what looks like an abandoned house. Inside, she discovers a Christmas that's been left behind—complete with faded decorations on a brittle Christmas tree and dusty stockings filled with loss. Someone spies smoke coming from the chimney of the empty house and alerts Dr. Luke Griffin, the owner. He rarely visits the home that harbors so many bittersweet memories for him. Then Luke meets Hope, and he knows this mother-to-be desperately needs help. With no room at any local inn, Luke invites Hope to stay, unaware of the danger following her. While running from the darkness, the embers of Christmas present are stirred with an unexpected birth and a holiday romance. But will Hope and Luke live to see a Christmas future?

Taken by Dark (coming soon)

CAPE THOMAS SERIES:

Dubiosity (**Book 1**)

Savannah Harris vowed to leave behind her old life as an investigative reporter. But when two migrant workers go missing, her curiosity spikes. As more eerie incidents begin afflicting the area, each works to draw Savannah out of her seclusion and raise the stakes—for her and the surrounding community. Even as Savannah's new boarder, Clive Miller, makes her feel things she thought long forgotten, she suspects he's hiding something too, and he's not the only one. As secrets emerge and danger closes in, Savannah must choose between faith and uncertainty. One wrong decision might spell the end . . . not just for her but for everyone around her. Will she unravel the mystery in time, or will doubt get the best of her?

Disillusioned (**Book 2**)

Nikki Wright is desperate to help her brother, Bobby, who hasn't been the same since escaping from a detainment camp run by terrorists in Colombia. Rumor has it that he betrayed his navy brothers and conspired with those who held him hostage, and both the press and the military are hounding him for answers. All Nikki wants is to shield her brother so he has time to recover and heal. But soon they realize the paparazzi are the least of their worries. When a group of men try to abduct Nikki and her brother, Bobby insists that Kade Wheaton, another former SEAL, can keep them out of harm's way. But can Nikki trust Kade? After all, the man who broke her heart eight years ago is anything but safe...Hiding out in a farmhouse on the Chesapeake Bay, Nikki finds her loyalties—and the remnants of her long-held faith—tested as she and Kade put aside their differences to keep Bobby's increasingly erratic behavior under wraps. But when Bobby disappears, Nikki will have to trust Kade completely if she wants to uncover the truth about a rumored conspiracy. Nikki's life—and the fate of the nation—depends on it.

Distorted (**Book 3**)

Mallory Baldwin is a survivor. A former victim of human trafficking, she's been given a second chance, yet not a night goes by that she doesn't remember being a slave to weapons dealer Dante Torres. Despite being afraid of the dark and wary of strangers, Mallory is trying to rebuild her life by turning her tragedy into redemption. To former Navy SEAL Tennyson Walker, Mallory seems nothing like the shattered woman he rescued two years ago, and he can't help but be inspired by her strength and resilience. So when a stalker suddenly makes Mallory vulnerable once again, Tennyson steps up as her bodyguard to keep her safe. Mallory and Tennyson's mutual attraction can't be ignored, but neither can Mallory's suspicion that Tennyson is keeping a terrible secret about her past. As the nightmare closes in, it's not only Mallory and Tennyson's love that comes under fire but their very lives as well. Will their faith sustain them? Or will the darkness win once and for all?

STANDALONES:

The Good Girl

Tara Lancaster can sing "Amazing Grace" in three harmonies, two languages, and interpret it for the hearing impaired. She can list the Bible canon backward, forward, and alphabetized. The only time she ever missed church was when she had pneumonia and her mom made her stay home. Then her life shatters and her reputation is left in ruins. She flees halfway across the country to dog-sit, but the quiet anonymity she needs isn't waiting at her sister's house. Instead, she finds a knife with a threatening message, a fame-hungry friend, a too-hunky neighbor, and evidence of . . . a ghost? Following all the rules has gotten her nowhere. And nothing she learned in Sunday School can tell her where to go from there.

Death of the Couch Potato's Wife (**Suburban Sleuth Mysteries**)

You haven't seen desperate until you've met Laura

Berry, a career-oriented city slicker turned suburbanite housewife. Well-trained in the big-city commandment, "mind your own business," Laura is persuaded by her spunky seventy-year-old neighbor, Babe, to check on another neighbor who hasn't been seen in days. She finds Candace Flynn, wife of the infamous "Couch King," dead, and at last has a reason to get up in the morning. Someone is determined to stop her from digging deeper into the death of her neighbor, but Laura is just as determined to figure out who is behind the death-by-poisoned-pork-rinds.

Imperfect

Since the death of her fiancé two years ago, novelist Morgan Blake's life has been in a holding pattern. She has a major case of writer's block, and a book signing in the mountain town of Perfect sounds as perfect as its name. Her trip takes a wrong turn when she's involved in a hit-and-run: She hit a man, and he ran from the scene. Before fleeing, he mouthed the word "Help." First she must find him. In Perfect, she finds a small town that offers all she ever wanted. But is something sinister going on behind its cheery exterior? Was she invited as a guest of honor simply to do a book signing? Or was she lured to town for another purpose —a deadly purpose?

THE GABBY ST. CLAIRE DIARIES:

A TWEEN MYSTERY SERIES

The Curtain Call Caper (**Book 1**)

Is a ghost haunting the Oceanside Middle School auditorium? What else could explain the disasters surrounding the play—everything from missing scripts to a falling spotlight and damaged props? Seventh-grader Gabby St. Claire has dreamed about being part of her school's musical, but a series of unfortunate events threatens to shut down the production. While trying to uncover the culprit and save her fifteen minutes of fame, she also has to manage impossible teachers, cliques, her dysfunctional family, and a secret she can't tell even her best friend. Will Gabby figure out who or what is sabotaging the show . . . or will it be curtains for her and the rest of the cast?

The Disappearing Dog Dilemma (**Book 2**)

Why are dogs disappearing around town? When two friends ask seventh-grader Gabby St. Claire for her help in finding their missing canines, Gabby decides to unleash her sleuthing skills to sniff out whoever is behind the act. But time management and relationships get tricky as worrisome weather, a part-time job, and a new crush interfere with Gabby's investigation. Will her determination crack the case? Or will shadowy villains, a penchant for overcommitting, and even her own heart put her in the doghouse?

The Bungled Bike Burglaries (Book 3)

Stolen bikes and a long-forgotten time capsule leave one amateur sleuth baffled and busy. Seventh-grader Gabby St. Claire is determined to bring a bike burglar to justice—and not just because mean girl Donabell Bullock is strong-arming her. But each new clue brings its own set of trouble. As if that's not enough, Gabby finds evidence of a decades-old murder within the contents of the time capsule, but no one seems to take her seriously. As her investigation heats up, will Gabby's knack for being in the wrong place at the wrong time with the wrong people crack the case? Or will it prove hazardous to her health?

COMPLETE BOOK LIST:

Squeaky Clean Mysteries:
    #1 Hazardous Duty
    #2 Suspicious Minds
    #2.5 It Came Upon a Midnight Crime (a novella)
    #3 Organized Grime
    #4 Dirty Deeds
    #5 The Scum of All Fears
    #6 To Love, Honor, and Perish
    #7 Mucky Streak
    #8 Foul Play
    #9 Broom and Gloom
    #10 Dust and Obey
    #11 Thrill Squeaker
    #11.5 Swept Away (a novella)
    #12 Cunning Attractions
    #13 Clean Getaway

Squeaky Clean Companion Novella:
    While You Were Sweeping

The Sierra Files:

The Gabby St. Claire Diaries (a Tween Mystery series):

The Worst Detective Ever

Holly Anna Paladin Mysteries:

#5 Random Acts of Fraud

Carolina Moon Series:
Home Before Dark
Gone By Dark
Wait Until Dark
Light the Dark
Taken by Dark (coming September 2017)

Suburban Sleuth Mysteries:
#1 Death of the Couch Potato's Wife

Standalone Romantic-Suspense:
Keeping Guard
The Last Target
Race Against Time
Ricochet
Key Witness
Lifeline
High-Stakes Holiday Reunion
Desperate Measures
Hidden Agenda
Mountain Hideaway
Dark Harbor
Shadow of Suspicion
The Baby Assignment (coming January 2018)

Cape Thomas Series:

Dubiosity
Disillusioned
Distorted

Standalone Romantic Mystery:
The Good Girl

Suspense:
Imperfect
The Wrecking (coming in October)

Nonfiction:
Changed: True Stories of Finding God through Christian Music

The Novel in Me: The Beginner's Guide to Writing and Publishing a Novel

ABOUT THE AUTHOR

USA Today has called Christy Barritt's books "scary, funny, passionate, and quirky."

Christy writes both mystery and romantic suspense novels that are clean with underlying messages of faith. Her books have won the Daphne du Maurier Award for Excellence in Suspense and Mystery, have been twice nominated for the Romantic Times Reviewers' Choice Award, and have finaled for both a Carol Award and Foreword Magazine's Book of the Year.

She is married to her Prince Charming, a man who thinks she's hilarious—but only when she's not trying to be. Christy is a self-proclaimed klutz, an avid music lover who's known for spontaneously bursting into song, and a road trip aficionado.

When she's not working or spending time with her family, she enjoys singing, playing the guitar, and exploring small, unsuspecting towns where people have no idea how accident-prone she is.

Find Christy online at:
www.christybarritt.com
www.facebook.com/christybarritt
www.twitter.com/cbarritt

Sign up for Christy's newsletter to get information on all of her latest releases here:
www.christybarritt.com/newsletter-sign-up/

If you enjoyed this book, please consider leaving a review.

Made in the USA
Columbia, SC
26 November 2017